UNRELENTING

The Man Who Turned a Local Recycling Push,
Into a National Plastic Ban

DON WOODSTOCK

Verdict

Unrelenting by Don Woodstock is more than a memoir. It's a movement. From rural Jamaica to Winnipeg's City Hall, Woodstock chronicles his fight for environmental reform with honesty, grit, and impact. This isn't just a personal journey, it's the true account of how grassroots persistence helped drive a national plastic ban.

What sets this book apart is its fusion of emotional authenticity with strategic insight. Whether he's singing in City Hall or changing public language, Woodstock shows how heart and strategy work together to influence policy. His lived experience, grounded in dual cultural identity, gives the story global resonance.

Beneath each chapter lie subtle, deliberately placed dots, themes, metaphors, and moments that encourage the reader to engage thoughtfully. The parable of "carrying water in a basket" becomes a guiding metaphor for tackling impossible tasks with creativity and resolve. Renaming "Garbage Day" as "Recycle Day" reflects his understanding that even small shifts in language can spark broader cultural change. The book doesn't deliver easy answers. It invites deep reflection.

Real-world imagery—like plastic bags tangled in city trees—adds a visual urgency that forces the reader to confront everyday neglect. His letter to the next generation doesn't preach; it passes the torch.

Unrelenting isn't just inspiring—it's a working model for change. Woodstock offers more than a story—he delivers a roadmap. In today's climate-conscious world, this book arrives with truth, timing, and undeniable power.

Table of Contents

Acknowledgements

No movement begins with just one man. It may begin with a thought, a conviction, or a singular voice, but it only grows and blooms when others dare to believe in the vision and lend their hands to lift the weight. The journey that this book captures—my life's work of service, advocacy, and environmental passion—was never walked alone. It is because of the love, mentorship, resistance, and support I received from others that I have been able to remain steadfast on this long, winding path. To every person who stood by me—whether for a season or for the entire journey—I extend my most sincere, boundless gratitude.

I would like to thank **Sobey's Grocery Store** for their early and bold decision to eliminate plastic bags. It was not just a commercial choice; it was a moral one that changed the landscape of consumer responsibility in Canada. That one corporate stance gave validation to the work I had been doing for years—proof that vision and action can meet, and something good can happen when they do.

To **Dr. David Suzuki**, thank you for your counsel, your endorsement, and your faith in the power of grassroots change. Your voice and your life's work have been a north star to many of us. For your words of encouragement when I needed them most, I am eternally grateful. You reminded me that change begins locally and grows outward like ripples in a pond.

To **Minister Jim Rondeau**, **Dr. Jon Gerard**, and **Debra Green**, you opened doors, heard my proposals, and gave me your time and your support. Thank you for believing that the environment was worth fighting for, and for helping me make real progress where bureaucracy often stalled.

To **Mr. Randy Parks** of the Winnipeg Water & Waste Department and **Emterra Environmental**, your invaluable assistance gave shape to the infrastructure behind the vision. Ideas mean little without execution, and your expertise helped bring life to what was once just a dream.

To my babies, **Aspyn and Julien**, you are the heartbeat of this mission. Your eyes are the ones I imagine when I think about what this planet will look like in fifty years. Your laughter, your questions, your love—they reminded me daily that what I'm fighting for is bigger than me.

To **Matt Cundle from Power 97**, thank you for taking the time to listen. Your platform became a launching pad for one of the most meaningful environmental shifts in this city's history. To **Mayor Sam Katz**, who served Winnipeg from 2004 to 2014—thank you for casting the deciding vote that helped us move from "Garbage Day" to "Recycle Day." Your courage to vote with vision instead of convenience will always stand out.

To **Allan Sayegh** and **Jeremy Vallance from Shaw Cable**, thank you for lending your skills and your cameras to tell the stories that needed telling. Through film and broadcast, we helped educate a city and inspire communities beyond our borders.

To the late **Harvey Smith**, your encouraging report to City Hall and your unwavering support of progressive environmental initiatives will never be forgotten. You stood with me when few did, and I remain grateful.

To **Keenan Darling**, thank you for capturing the essence and energy of the first Plastic Bag Day with your photography. Your lens preserved a moment that history will remember.

To **Wally Ruben**, my dear friend—your advice, your support, and even your spaghetti dinner helped nourish the mind and soul during some of the hardest days of this journey.

To my wife, my rock, my confidante—**Kathy Harris**—there are not enough pages in this book to express what your love has meant to me. You have supported me through every uphill climb, every setback, every win. You saw the man before the headlines and helped build him brick by brick with your faith in me. You are not just acknowledged; you are etched into every chapter of this work.

Each person mentioned here has left an indelible mark on this journey. I thank you not just for your contribution, but for showing me that I was never alone. When the world said no, you gave me a reason to say yes again.

And to every soul who has ever picked up a piece of trash, recycled a bottle, turned off a light to save energy, or simply taught their children to respect nature—this book is for you too. You are the movement. You are the miracle.

Let this book serve as a reminder that when people stand together for something bigger than themselves, change is not only possible—it is inevitable.

Introduction

In the heart of Winnipeg, where bustling city life meets the pied pipers of nature, a fateful story unfolds.

Over the past twenty-four years, Winnipeg has been a city in flux, transforming with each passing day. But standing firmly in the background of genuine urban progress is a persistent hero—a man who has made it his mission to ensure the city not only grows economically and politically but also flourishes with its natural resources. Picture a person embraced by this city since the year 2000, whose passion for community leadership and environmental activism knows no bounds.

This figure is my husband, Don Woodstock. And what he has done for this city cannot be captured in mere headlines. It lives in every child who now knows to toss a bottle in the blue bin. It lives in every parent who brings a reusable bag to the store. It lives in every conversation that begins with, "What can we do to make things better?"

Don has dedicated himself to nurturing the very soul of this city, pouring into Winnipeg the kind of energy and love that most reserve for their own family—and in many ways, this city has become his family. His vision? A Winnipeg that wears bold shades of green, where sustainability isn't just policy—it's practice. A city that breathes life into its citizens as much as they breathe life into it. A city that future generations can inherit not with hesitation, but with pride.

This journey began in earnest in 2001 when Don first urged Manitoba Liberal Party leader Dr. Jon Gerard to consider banning plastic bags. At the time, the proposal was bold—some said impossible. But Don never believed in impossible. By 2007, the momentum was growing, and in 2008 he stood before Winnipeg City Hall's Executive Policy Committee, where he secured a majority vote to rename 'Garbage Day' to 'Recycle Day'—a symbolic shift that would change hearts, habits, and ultimately, the landscape of the city.

That moment wasn't just a victory—it was a seed. And like all great seeds, it grew. A series of events were set in motion. The city's environmental conscience was stirred, and for the first time in a long time, people began to believe that meaningful change was not only necessary but possible.

But saving a city, building a movement, and securing a healthy legacy for our children is no small operation. It takes courage. It takes relentless effort. It takes a man willing to be misunderstood, challenged, and even mocked—all for the sake of what is right. Don has proven time and again that he will stop at nothing to bring his vision to life—a vision of a city that leads, that lives with intention, that doesn't just exist but thrives in harmony with nature.

His fight wasn't for recognition—it was for restoration. It was for the right of every Winnipegger to live in a city that values the Earth beneath its streets and the air above its skyline. He fought to put integrity back into policy, to put action behind ideals.

This book is not just about the battles he's fought or the policies he's helped shape. It is about belief—his belief that one person, when driven by purpose and guided by love, can indeed change the world around him.

To know Don is to know a man who sees beyond what is and works tirelessly for what could be. His legacy is already being written, not in plaques or politics, but in the lives of those inspired to live a little greener, a little braver, and a whole lot more consciously.

It has been my absolute honour to walk alongside him, to witness his devotion firsthand, and to now introduce to you the story of the man I know best—Unrelenting.

—Kathy Harris, *a proud, loving wife*

Prologue

I was born in St. Elizabeth, Jamaica, and raised on a farm by my grandfather. It was the early 1970s, where the sun never seemed to sleep, and the land dictated our rhythm. Farming was not just a way of life—it was *life itself*. Everything we did flowed from the soil, and every lesson I needed to learn was planted in that earth. What some may have seen as hardship, I came to understand as discipline, resourcefulness, and spiritual preparation for something greater.

A typical Jamaican rural home with a hardworking Jamaican farmer harvesting yam.

I found that most of the values I carry with me today stem from my grandfather's peculiar requests—small acts of obedience that carried big meaning. The only thing he probably never asked of me was to turn sand into water. But, in hindsight, you'll see how the seemingly impossible became possible, and how the simplest lessons earned me a life of purpose in a country thousands of miles from where I was born.

Farming life wasn't romantic. It was demanding. But I learned sustainability from necessity. I learned how to respect every drop of water, how to preserve energy before we ever had light switches, and how to live in harmony with the land, not above it. These lessons shaped not only my character, but also my worldview. I learned that nature is not a resource to be exploited—it is a partner to be protected.

One day, my grandfather handed me a woven basket and told me to fetch water from the river which was a main source of water for our home. A basket not having holes would be like a leopard not having spots. I thought he had finally lost it. But when you're a boy in a Jamaican household, you don't talk back—you act. So off I went, feeling foolish, but committed.

I spent hours trying to retain water in that basket. As the sun dipped low and fear of duppies (ghosts) lurking behind every banana tree and leaf that moved, and every toad & insect that made its nightly call crept in as if someone was always right behind you every moment. I started to make my way home, feeling defeated, when my grandfather appeared. Without a word, he took three large cocoa leaves and placed them in the basket, sealing the gaps. He dipped it into the water, and to my amazement, it held. Had it not been so practical, it might have seemed like magic.

He looked me straight in the eye. "Was this task bigger than you?" he asked. I whispered, "No." He didn't smile, didn't console. He simply walked away, as if to say, "Lesson delivered."

That single moment rooted itself in my heart. Since that day, I've carried water in a basket—not literally, but metaphorically. I came to understand that when the world tells you something can't be done, you don't give up. You seek out the wisdom of someone who's walked that road before. You keep trying. You adapt. You persist. Because the solution is often just one leaf away.

This belief has become the cornerstone of my journey in Canada. When I arrived in Winnipeg, I brought that same basket with me—the one filled with determination, resourcefulness, and a refusal to see impossibility. It is with that spirit I began rallying for environmental change in this city.

When I stood in front of City Hall and urged them to rename "Garbage Day" to "Recycle Day," many saw me as a joke. Some spat racist slurs in my direction and questioned if someone who looked like me could ever be taken seriously in Canadian politics. But I wasn't deterred. Not because I'm fearless, but because I knew I wasn't alone. My grandfather's wisdom was still whispering through me. And I knew that if I kept showing up, kept placing those metaphorical leaves in the right places, something would eventually hold.

You see, this mission has never been just about recycling or plastic bags. It's about how we see ourselves. Do we believe we are too small to make a difference? Or do we realize that each of us carries the potential to be the missing piece in someone else's impossible task?

This book chronicles my journey from the red dirt of Jamaica to the snowy streets of Winnipeg, from one impossible task to the next. It is a testament to perseverance, to faith, and to the power of community. The road hasn't been easy, but every challenge has only deepened my gratitude—for my family, my mentors, and the countless people who finally said yes after years of hearing no.

This isn't just my story. This is the story of anyone who has ever tried to carry water in a basket—and found a way.

Chapter 1

The Beginning | The birth of a
Local activist and Community leader

In 1995, I immigrated to Canada in my early twenties. Like many who make the journey from Jamaica to a new land, I carried with me a suitcase filled with little more than ambition, a few clothes, and the echoes of my grandfather's lessons etched into every fibre of my being. I was born in St. Elizabeth, raised in the bosom of the earth, on a farm that taught me everything I needed to know about life: discipline, sacrifice, and how to take only what you need while giving back what you can. Farming wasn't simply a chore; it was a spiritual transaction. What you sow, you reap—not only in the soil, but in your actions, your integrity, and your heart.

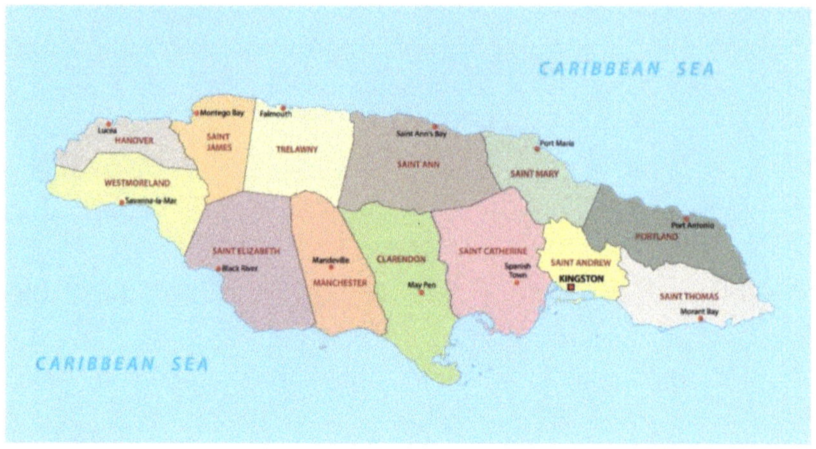

Toronto was my first stop. It was bustling, cold, indifferent—and at first, unforgiving. I started working as a salesman for American Data & Telecommunications (ADT) selling home alarm systems. Thirty days. That's how long it took me to make my first sale. Thirty days of rejection, slammed doors, and people looking through me like I didn't exist. But the day that first customer said yes, something inside me shifted. The tides turned, and I began to see myself differently. That moment taught me that failure is never final unless you make it so. I became the national sales trainer for the largest outfit doing alarm sales in Canada. The immigrant kid with a Jamaican accent becomes a teacher. "Right Jason & Carl?"

But my spirit was restless. There was something calling me westward. In November 1999, I moved to Winnipeg—a place known more for its biting winters than its warm welcomes. I remember stepping off the plane into a wall of cold that nearly knocked the breath out of me. Yet somehow, I knew this was where I was meant to be. It was in this city that the revolution of 'Don Woodstock' would take root. I didn't just want to survive here. I wanted to leave footprints. I wanted to matter.

I wore many hats in those early years—real estate agent, caterer, filmmaker, TV personality. But every role I stepped into seemed to point me in one clear direction: service. I began to recognize the deep connection between environmental injustice and community neglect. I saw how the way we treated our neighbourhoods was a direct reflection of how we treated ourselves. I realized that the environment wasn't some abstract concept reserved for scientists and politicians—it was the air our kids breathe, the water we drink, the streets we walk.

Winnipeg became my canvas. It was here I began to shape the vision I had carried since Jamaica: to build a better, greener, more sustainable environment, one action at a time. The turning point came when I started pushing for a small but powerful change—renaming "Garbage Day" to "Recycle Day." To most, it was semantics. But I knew that names carry meaning. When we shift language, we shift mindset. And when we shift mindset, we create momentum. What people discard reflects what they value. By elevating the idea of recycling, I wanted to help people see waste not as an end, but as a beginning.

When I stood alone on the streets of Winnipeg, rallying for this change, there was no applause. No media coverage. No fanfare. People sneered. They called me crazy. Some called me worse. I remember a man spitting at my feet and asking if I truly believed someone like *me* could do anything meaningful for this city. That moment burned. Not because it wounded me—but because it revealed the uphill climb ahead.

But I didn't flinch. I was used to resistance. Resistance, after all, is confirmation that you're pressing against something that needs to move.

Why plastic bags? Why bother? I'll tell you why. Plastic bags were the symbol of a bigger sickness—our culture of convenience, waste, and environmental amnesia. I knew that targeting something so simple, so pervasive, would force people to stop and think. And thinking is the first step toward change.

In 2006, I started organizing towards my goal by talking to people, getting out into the community more and building the connections needed. This was a momentum builder. In 2008, I stood in front of Winnipeg's Executive Policy Committee at City Hall, and for the first time, I saw real progress. The committee voted in favour of the name change. It was a moment that felt like electricity in my veins—proof that persistence pays off.

Not long after, we organized Winnipeg's first International Day to Ban Plastic Bags. Over 44,000 plastic bags were collected and exchanged for reusable totes. I watched hundreds of people show up—not because they were forced, but because they *wanted* to. Because someone finally said: "This matters!"

I began to see a shift. Retailers started taking notice. Kildonan Place and Polo Park Shopping Centre jumped on board. What began as a one-man push became a movement.

And yet, the fight was far from over. As the saying goes, "The darkest part of the night is just before the dawn." But I never doubted. Because if we can change minds, we can change habits. And if we change habits, we change the future.

This chapter was only the beginning. The birth of a local activist? Yes. But more importantly, it was the birth of a lifelong commitment— to serve, to speak truth to power, and to never let silence take the place of action.

If you're reading this now, know that you, too, have a part to play. You don't need permission. You just need passion. Because even a whisper can start an avalanche—if it's honest, relentless, and rooted in love.

Chapter 2

A Fateful collaboration | U, Me and the Environment

Take a moment and envision a world where the streets gleam with cleanliness, not because someone was paid to clean them, but because people made a conscious decision not to litter. Picture neighbourhoods where compost bins sit proudly on porches, solar panels grace rooftops, and recycling isn't an afterthought—it's second nature. Now stop and ask yourself: what's your role in creating that world?

This question became my life's compass.

My message has always been simple: we cannot live healthy lives in sick environments. And we cannot fix broken systems unless we first open our eyes to our own behaviours. The work of environmental activism starts not in policy chambers or newsrooms, but in homes, in schools, and in front of the mirror.

That was the heartbeat behind the television project I co-produced with Shaw Cable: *U, Me and the Environment*. The title says it all. This wasn't just about government responsibility or corporate accountability. It was about us—*you*, *me*, and the daily choices we make that ripple through the world around us.

I remember the first time I stood on camera for that series. My mind raced with questions: Would people care? Would they listen? Would they finally *see* what I had been shouting about for years? But I pushed forward because I knew that if we could just get people to think differently about the things they touched every day, we could ignite change from the inside out.

So, we started small. We walked people through their morning routines—shampoo, deodorant, body wash, makeup—and explained the hidden cost behind those everyday products. Not in dollars, but in damage. You see, we rarely consider that these personal items—so casually applied—can be filled with chemicals derived from petrochemicals, the byproducts of oil and gas.

Take *parabens* for example. They're in your lotion, your moisturizer, your soap. Cheap preservatives, sure. But dangerous? Absolutely. Parabens disrupt hormones. They've been linked to early puberty in young girls and fibroid development in children. Yes—*children*. This isn't fearmongering. This is fact. And most of us had no idea.

That's why we had to make the invisible visible. We had to show people that environmentalism isn't just about forests and oceans—it's about our bodies, our health, and our families. Every product we use, every package we unwrap, every item we toss in the trash, sends a message: either we're part of the solution, or we're part of the problem.

People often ask, "Don, what made you care so much?" The truth is, I didn't have the luxury of ignorance. In 2001, I was invited on a tour of northern communities in Manitoba with Dr. Jon Gerard, and what I saw shook me to my core. Entire neighbourhoods overwhelmed by pollution. Garbage littering roadsides. Children growing up with no access to clean drinking water while mines loomed in the background. It wasn't just disturbing—it was enraging.

And in the middle of that garbage? Plastic bags. Always the plastic bags.

That trip changed something in me. It stripped away any illusions I had about the environmental crisis being far away or someone else's problem. This was *our* backyard. Our neighbours. Our country. And I knew right then that if I didn't speak out, I would become complicit in the silence.

So, I leaned harder into the work. I made *U, Me and the Environment* not as a vanity project, but as a vessel—a way to translate science into street language, policy into personal action. And it worked. People started paying attention. Families started asking questions. Consumers began checking labels.

But the lesson that humbled me most was this: awareness without action is just noise. If we want people to change their behaviours, we need to show them how. Not shame them but equip them. That's why the show didn't stop at warnings—we offered solutions. We highlighted alternative products. We introduced viewers to green companies and wellness experts. We connected the dots between personal wellness and environmental stewardship.

Green living isn't just a slogan. It's a worldview. A declaration that we can live differently, eat differently, shop differently, and still lead full, happy, and meaningful lives. And Winnipeg—despite its slow start—had the bones to become a leader in sustainability. We had 95% renewable energy, we had the space, we had the brains. What we needed was the *will.*

That's what I've tried to build through every episode, every speech, every interview. A will to act. A will to care. A will to look past the noise and realize that the world we leave behind is the world our children must live in.

There's a Jamaican proverb I love: *"One, one cocoa full basket."* Meaning, small efforts add up. That's how we build change—bit by bit, voice by voice, step by step. Whether it's a single person switching to a soap made from renewable material or an entire city banning plastic bags, every act counts.

U, Me and the Environment was not just a show—it was a spark. A collaboration between my heart, the community, and the truth that when we care for ourselves, we naturally begin to care for the planet. Because we're not separate from nature—we *are* nature.

And if we are to survive, we must protect ourselves by protecting the very Earth that sustains us. That begins with you. That begins with me. And that begins—now.

Chapter 3

A Friend indeed | The David Suzuki Foundation & Debra Green

When my daughter Aspyn was either three or four years old, I overheard her telling her little brother, "You have to put it in the recycling bin first before you know it was supposed to go into the garbage." It made me laugh—not because she was wrong, but because she had distilled my entire philosophy into one childlike sentence. In her innocent logic was a powerful truth: we must always try to save something before we decide to discard it. That is how we should treat objects—and people's ideas.

That moment reminded me why I began this journey in the first place. It wasn't to get famous. It wasn't to win elections. It was to plant something meaningful for the next generation to inherit. I wasn't doing this for headlines—I was doing it for *her* and for every child who will one day ask, "Why didn't someone do something sooner?"

But the truth is, no one saw my vision in the early days. It was a lonely, uphill climb. I knocked on doors that were slammed in my face. I was called a nuisance, a distraction, even delusional. There were people—some in power, others just passing by—who told me to "go back to my country," and asked, with thinly veiled contempt, what made me think I could change *anything* in Canada. But what they didn't know was that my backbone was built on Jamaican farm soil. And my purpose? Bigger than any insult they could throw.

Still, no one can fight alone forever. Even the strongest need allies. And when those allies show up—not just to pat you on the back, but to stand in the mud with you—it changes everything. That's what happened when I crossed paths with the **David Suzuki Foundation** and later, **Debra Green**, the general manager of Polo Park Shopping Centre. They weren't just supporters. They were catalysts.

Dr. David Suzuki is one of the few voices in this country who speaks about the environment with both scientific clarity and moral authority. So, when I was told I'd be meeting him in 2007, my heart raced. I wasn't meeting a celebrity—I was meeting a kindred spirit. Someone who understood that the fight for the environment is ultimately a fight for *human dignity*. That year, I had already been working on my first documentary, *Your World and Mine*, highlighting environmental neglect in Winnipeg. I was pitching Shaw, rallying City Hall, and visiting northern communities with Dr. Jon Gerard to document the poverty and pollution that rarely made the news. But meeting Dr. Suzuki? That lit a fire under me I didn't know I needed.

"Start at the local level and don't stop," he told me. "Sooner or later, someone will listen to you."

Those words became a fuel line to my soul. Because here was a man who had seen it all, who had faced his own share of resistance, telling *me* to keep going. And I did. I returned home from that meeting with renewed vigour, finishing *Your World and Mine* and hand-delivering it to media outlets, City Hall, the provincial legislature—anyone who would listen. I didn't have a marketing team. I didn't have a campaign budget. What I had was a message and a mission.

Ian Hanington, the communications specialist at the David Suzuki Foundation at the time, once said, "What Don Woodstock has accomplished speaks to the power of the individual." And hearing those words felt like years of struggle had finally found their echo.

In 2010, the David Suzuki Foundation came out with its 'Finding Solutions' magazine, and what do you know, I was featured as a Community Leader for my advocacy here in the city. I was elated to say the least to be honoured by the premier environmental group in Canada.

Then there was **Debra Green**. If you don't know her name, you should. In a time when most corporate leaders were looking the other way, Debra leaned in. As general manager of one of Winnipeg's largest shopping centres, she could have chosen to stay neutral. Instead, she became a champion.

The big retailers weren't budging. They were profiting enormously from the sale of plastic bags—a product with one of the highest profit margins in the store. A few cents to make, and they'd charge five or ten times that at checkout. It was low-hanging fruit for corporate greed. But Debra invited me to a meeting of major grocery store executives. I wasn't even scheduled to speak. But she *made space* for me. That's what leaders do—they make room where there is none.

I told them, "Give me one day. One single day where you don't hand out plastic bags. One day to show the people a better way."

And they gave it to me.

That single day turned into the first *Reusable Bag Day*, a citywide movement that saw malls and grocery stores handing out reusable totes, educating shoppers, and shifting behaviour in real time. We gave away thousands of bags and collected even more plastic ones. What started as a desperate plea became a public success. And from that spark, we saw the federal government take steps towards a national ban on plastic bags.

If you think one voice can't make a difference, let me tell you this: one voice teamed with the right ally becomes a *chorus*. And a chorus can shake buildings.

Debra Green didn't have to listen. Dr. Suzuki didn't have to encourage. Ian Hanington didn't have to speak on my behalf. But they did. And I'll never forget it. Because sometimes, all a movement needs is someone to say, "I see you. Keep going."

And to those of you reading this—be that someone. Open the door. Make the introduction. Invite the underdog to speak. Because you never know when your simple act of belief will help change the future.

And to Dr. Suzuki, Ian, Debra, and everyone else who stood beside me in the shadows when there was no spotlight—I thank you. Your belief gave birth to action. And your action helped birth a revolution.

Don Woodstock speaks with Dr. David Suzuki

Chapter 4

The world is in our hands | Your World and Mine

Fight the Plastic Bags
–
It's Your World and Mine

Let's Recycle!

Martin, the drummer and Don discussing what could be done for recycling garbage.

"It's your world, as much as it is mine."

That was the phrase I uttered repeatedly during the filming of *Your World and Mine*. And each time I said it, I meant it even more than the last. Because the world doesn't belong to politicians or corporations or activists alone. It belongs to *all of us*. That's the core message that I carried with me when I stepped in front of the camera to host one of the most meaningful projects of my life.

The year was 2007. Winnipeg was waking up—slowly, unevenly, but undeniably—to the idea that how we treat the environment reflects how we value ourselves. I had already spent years knocking on doors, rallying support, and fighting uphill battles to make the words "Recycle Day" part of our civic vocabulary. And while the policies and votes were critical, I knew something was missing: connection. People needed to see *themselves* in the story. Not as spectators, but as protagonists.

That's when the idea for **Your World and Mine** took hold.

I partnered with filmmaker and visionary Martin Knispel, a man who shared my desire to turn the camera not on the problems alone, but on

16

the people. The everyday folks in Winnipeg who were already doing the work, the residents who cared deeply but didn't always know how to act, and the skeptics who needed one more reason to believe.

We didn't start with a million-dollar budget or big production houses. We started with a dream and a borrowed microphone. I walked the streets of Winnipeg—interviewing residents, stopping by festivals, talking to business owners, and sitting down with property managers who were testing out new recycling initiatives in apartment complexes. The most powerful moments were the simplest ones: an elderly woman explaining how she reuses jars instead of tossing them, a teenager picking up litter outside his school, a family proudly showing off their compost pile.

And then there were the heartbreaking stories—people living in areas where garbage bins were scarce, where recycling resources hadn't yet reached, and where the only "education" came from trial and error. It wasn't fair. It wasn't right. But it was real. And we needed to expose it.

One interview that stuck with me was a resident who commented that every major public event—whether a street festival, outdoor concert, or cultural gathering—left behind a massive trail of trash. "It's like we celebrate for a few hours and then leave the city to clean up our mess," he said with a chuckle, masking a real sense of shame.

That struck a nerve. It wasn't just about policies—it was about pride. We needed people to *care* about their communities in the same way they cared about their own front yard. But how could we expect them to care if no one had ever asked them to? *Your World and Mine* became that invitation.

A highlight of the documentary was our visit to 33 Hargrave Street, an apartment complex with 254 units—managed by none other than my good friend, Wally Ruben. In collaboration with the city, we distributed blue recycling bins to each unit. Within just a month, the volume of garbage collected had dropped by 35–40%. People responded positively. Why? Because they were given the *tools* to do the right thing.

Don Woodstock and Wally Ruben speaks about recycling in his apartment building.

That's a lesson I've carried with me ever since: most people want to do the right thing. They just need the means and the message. And sometimes, they need a nudge—a reminder that they are not powerless.

You can see the story unfold for yourself. Part 1 and Part 2 of *Your World and Mine* are still on YouTube, for anyone who wants to witness what real people with limited resources, but big hearts can accomplish. And I'll never forget Wally's face when he saw the change that took place at Hargrave. "Don," he said, "this is what partnership looks like."

What we proved in that moment was something that still holds true today: when people are informed, equipped, and respected, they rise. When you give people bins, knowledge, and encouragement, they don't just recycle more—they believe more. They begin to understand that their actions matter.

But awareness alone wasn't enough. The city needed to match the energy of its people. In 2010, the Manitoba Multi-Material Stewardship Program (now known as SimplyRecycle) was created to centralize recycling education and infrastructure. I remember being proud—and a little disappointed. Because despite having fought tooth and nail for that very message, I was never invited to participate in the initiative I had championed for so long even though I repeatedly asked.

But I didn't let that deter me. I had never done this for applause. I did it because I believed—and still believe—that Winnipeg can lead the world in environmental consciousness if it simply embraces its own potential.

A 2021 survey reinforced everything I had already seen firsthand. Seventy-one percent of respondents reported they always recycle. And yet, barriers remained: confusion about what items are recyclable, a lack of clear instructions, and skepticism about whether their recyclables were even being processed. The truth is, many still believe their efforts are in vain. That they sort diligently, rinse containers, and haul bins to the curb, only for it all to end up in a landfill.

That's not just discouraging. It's dangerous. Because if people stop believing in the system, they stop participating in it.

That's why *Your World and Mine* still matters. Because people need reminders that they are *not* alone, that their actions do matter, and that they are part of a broader movement toward a better world. This chapter isn't just about a documentary. It's about a philosophy. That *our* world— the one we share—is only as strong as the hands that care for it.

And those hands? They belong to *you*.

So, whether you're rinsing a bottle, starting a compost bin, or educating your children about waste—know that you are a steward of something sacred. This Earth. This city. This legacy.

Because it is your world—as much as it is mine.

Black plastic bags and yellow tape tangled in bare branches

Chapter 5

A Call to Action - A Song for The City

How do you walk back into City Hall after being ignored?

How do you speak again to a room full of decision-makers when you've already tried everything you could—facts, urgency, reason—and none of it moved the needle?

That was the question as I needed to answer for my presentation on February 18, 2009 for the Standing Policy Committee on Infrastructure Renewal and Public Works. I'd been advocating for years to change the way Winnipeg thought about waste. My push to rename "Garbage Day" to "Recycle Day" wasn't just about semantics—it was about psychology. It was about how language shapes action. But my words weren't landing. I could feel it.

So, I sat with the challenge. I prayed on it. And then, a thought passed through me like a whisper: *music.*

Music speaks to the soul when logic can't reach. That's what Bob Marley meant when he said, "One good thing about music, when it hits, you feel no pain." It pierces you, but it doesn't wound. It wakes something up inside of you. And that was exactly what this city needed—*a wake-up call.*

I kept thinking about a song I'd grown up hearing. A song filled with hope but also filled with challenge. A song recorded decades earlier, but one that spoke as if it had been written for *this exact moment in Winnipeg.* The message of the song was simple: we can no longer afford to sleep through the problems we face. The time has come for every segment of society—doctors, teachers, parents, children, politicians—to open their eyes and take responsibility. We all have a role in shaping the kind of world we leave behind.

The song by **Harold Melvin & The Blue Notes - Wake Up Everybody No more sleeping in bed,** spoke to me in a way that statistics never could.

And it gave me my answer.

So, when my time came to present, I stood in front of that committee, took a breath, and said just five words:

"Good morning, everyone. I'll begin."

Then I began to sing a Capella style "Wake Everybody, No More Sleeping In Bed" song.

No music. No instruments. No introduction. Just my voice. My faith. And a message carried through melody.

I was the first person to do my presentation in song in City Hall's history, and I didn't do it for attention. I did it because I *had to.* Because nothing else had worked. And because the city—our people—needed to be stirred awake.

What happened next still humbles me to this day.

I finished the song, and for a moment, there was silence. A rare thing in chambers. Then—applause. A full, genuine, human reaction. The message had landed. Not through policy language. Not through printed handouts. Through *feeling*. Through sound. Through something that bypassed argument and tapped directly into truth.

Later that day, the motion was officially presented. It proposed that all references in city materials be changed from "Garbage Day" to "Recycle Day." Councillor Mike Pagtakhan moved the motion, and Councillor Gord Steeves seconded it. There was a vote. And as fate would have it, the council split—dead even.

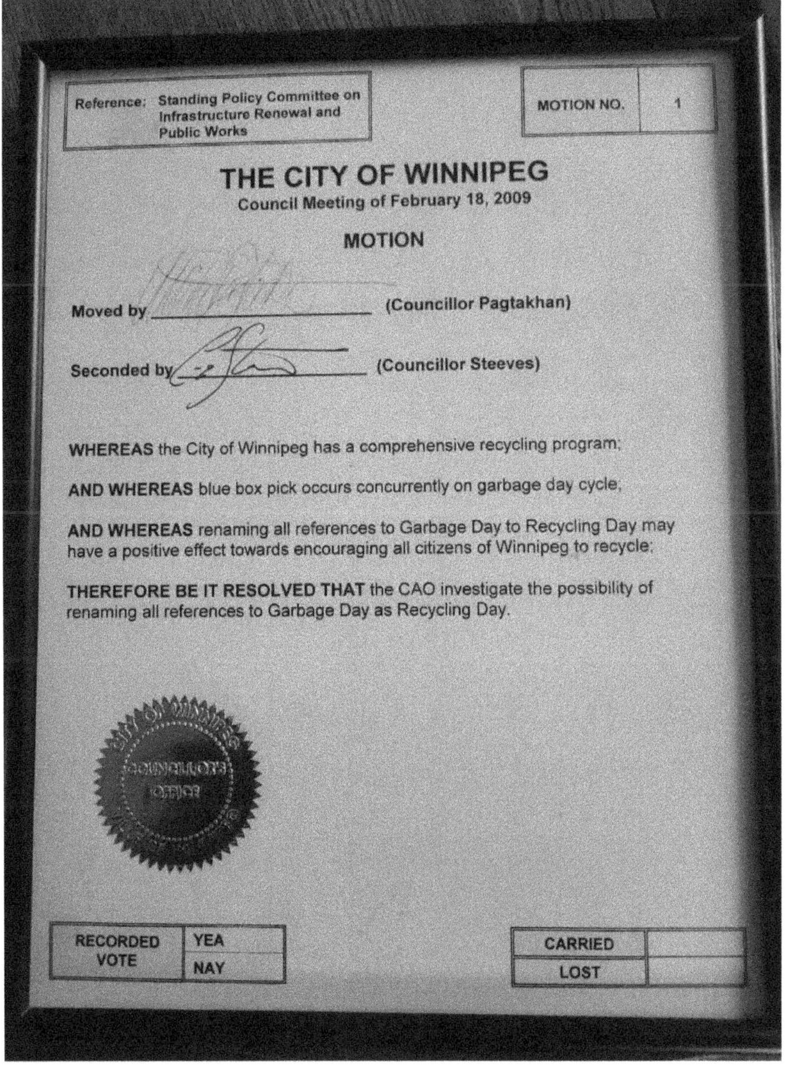

| Reference: Standing Policy Committee on Infrastructure Renewal and Public Works | MOTION NO. | 1 |

THE CITY OF WINNIPEG
Council Meeting of February 18, 2009

MOTION

Moved by _________________ (Councillor Pagtakhan)

Seconded by _________________ (Councillor Steeves)

WHEREAS the City of Winnipeg has a comprehensive recycling program;

AND WHEREAS blue box pick occurs concurrently on garbage day cycle;

AND WHEREAS renaming all references to Garbage Day to Recycling Day may have a positive effect towards encouraging all citizens of Winnipeg to recycle;

THEREFORE BE IT RESOLVED THAT the CAO investigate the possibility of renaming all references to Garbage Day as Recycling Day.

RECORDED VOTE	YEA		CARRIED	
	NAY		LOST	

The final decision came down to one man: Mayor Sam Katz.

And he said the words I'll never forget: *"It was the song that did it for me."*

That song—a decision I made from instinct, from conviction, from desperation—shifted the course of environmental history in Winnipeg. And it wasn't because I had a perfect voice. It was because I had the *right message*.

You see, the essence of that song wasn't about music at all. It was about *calling people to the moment*. It was about rising from our indifference. It was about acknowledging that change doesn't come from governments alone—it comes from all of us. Every neighbour who sorts their recyclables. Every teacher who explains the environment to their students. Every child who reminds their parents not to use plastic bags.

The song didn't ask for applause. It asked for *action*.

And in that moment, it got both.

Looking back, I realize now why the message was so powerful: because the truth doesn't have an expiration date. That song was written decades ago. But the message—that we must rise, pay attention, and work together for a better world—is eternal. It still resonates. It still calls. And it still challenges us.

Especially now.

At the time of that vote, Winnipeg was considered one of the worst cities in Canada for recycling. That's not an exaggeration—it's a fact. We were lagging, trapped in old habits and outdated systems. But changing the name from *Garbage Day* to *Recycle Day* did more than shift the language. It shifted *identity*. It reframed the conversation. It brought optimism where there was once resignation. It made people think differently about the blue bin at the end of their driveway.

Because when you emphasize what's *possible*, people respond.

And when you give them the tools—and the belief—they act.

To this day, I don't know exactly why that song came to me the way it did. Maybe it was divine timing. Maybe it was all the years of musical influence from my childhood. Maybe it was the culmination of frustration, passion, and hope. But I do know this: that moment was a *pivot*. Not just for the motion on the floor, but for my own journey as an advocate.

It reminded me that we don't always need louder arguments. Sometimes, we need deeper ones. Sometimes, we need to touch people—not just inform them.

And sometimes, we need to sing.

That morning in council wasn't just about recycling.

It was about reminding everyone that change is possible when we stop waiting for someone else to do it.

It was about telling Winnipeg, in the clearest and most human way I knew how, that we have more in common to recycle than we do to waste.

And all it took…was a song.

Chapter 6

Where we are today and where the
future needs to be

If you had told me back in 2001—when I first started knocking on doors and pushing the words "recycle" into public consciousness—that one day we would be measuring our landfill diversion by the ton and celebrating composting on a city-wide scale, I would have smiled with cautious hope. And then I would've said, "We're just getting started."

Let's be honest: Winnipeg hasn't always been the poster child for environmental responsibility. For years, we lagged other Canadian cities in both participation and infrastructure. But progress doesn't always come in sweeping declarations or dazzling headlines. Sometimes, it comes in small shifts, over time. And looking back, I'm proud to say: *we've moved the needle.*

With the introduction of the larger blue bins, Winnipeg's recycling participation saw a dramatic transformation. What had once lingered in the low 30% range surged to over 90%—a direct result of residents finally having the capacity to match their willingness to recycle. The bigger bins didn't just hold more materials—they unlocked the city's full potential to take sustainability seriously.

In the early 1990s, we barely had a recycling program. By 1995, curb side recycling began taking shape in single-family homes. It was a start—but far from enough. By the early 2000s, we saw the beginnings of recycling accessibility in multi-family residences. But for a city that prided itself on innovation, we were moving far too slow.

So, I did what I've always done. I kept pushing.

One of the proudest moments of my life was in 2012, when I stood in front of City Hall's Executive Policy Committee and lobbied not just for policy—but for perception. I asked them to change the name from "Garbage Day" to "Recycle Day" in 2008. It might have sounded trivial to some, but I knew the truth: words carry weight. When we call it garbage, we reinforce wastefulness. When we call it recycling, we plant the idea that value still exists.

It took two years of relentless lobbying to get that win for the name change. Then another two years to get the opportunity to present to the Executive Policy Committee for the bigger blue bins you see in your back lanes today. It was unanimous—and transformative. The name had changed. The bins were now to change. The conversation has changed.

The city had its so-called master plan—documents, diagrams, and carefully worded strategies—but it lacked vision. It lacked the kind of practical understanding that comes from paying attention to what ends up in people's bins, day after day. They talked about environmental goals in theory, but what they missed—what *everyone* had missed—was right there in our back lanes.

The truth was plain: we had *more recyclable material being thrown into garbage bins than actual garbage.* Over 70% of what Winnipeggers were sending to the landfill could have—and should have—been recycled. But the city had designed the system in reverse. Big black bins for garbage, and these tiny blue ones for recycling that overflowed within days. It wasn't just inefficient. It was upside down.

So, I took it upon myself to show them.

I met with then-Councillor Harvey Smith, a man who had a track record of giving voices like mine a fair hearing. From that meeting, I was given the opportunity to speak directly to City Council. My presentation—still available on YouTube by searching "Don Woodstock at Winnipeg City Hall - Recycling"—laid it all bare. I didn't just talk about hope and values. I came with *facts.*

I made the case that if we were serious about sustainability, we had to stop treating recycling like an afterthought. We needed infrastructure that matched our intentions. And we needed to fix the absurd mismatch between what people wanted to recycle and what they were able to fit into the bins provided.

That's when it clicked.

They realized what I had been saying all along: the system wasn't broken because people didn't care. It was broken because the city hadn't given them the proper tools.

And so, in **October 2012**, Winnipeg launched its **Cart Collection Program**. The city rolled out large, uniform carts for both garbage and recycling—finally giving residents the capacity they needed to participate meaningfully in the recycling effort. It was a turning point, not because it looked good on paper, but because it addressed a real, measurable problem.

It wasn't just some natural progression of policy.

It happened because I kept showing up. Because I told the truth. Because I presented a vision that forced decision-makers to confront just how backward the old system had been. The big blue bins were more than a container—they were an act of correction, a course change, a win built on persistence and proof.

And in that moment, Winnipeg began to align its words with its actions.

One bin at a time.

In recognition of his unwavering advocacy and vision, Don was presented with an honorary plaque for championing the name change from 'Garbage Day' to 'Recycle Day'—a milestone in Winnipeg's environmental journey. The plaque was awarded by Mayor Sam Katz, alongside Councillors Gord Steeves and Mike Pagtakhan, in acknowledgment of Don's role in reshaping how the city thinks about waste and sustainability.

City Councillor Mike Pagtakhan, Mayor Sam Katz, Don Woodstock and City Councillor Gord Steeves at Winnipeg's City Hall.

Mayor Sam Katz, Don Woodstock, with Aspyn and Julien Woodstock (daughter & son)

Alongside that, we saw the introduction of the **Yard Waste Collection program**, which now diverts over 30,000 tons of compostable material from landfills every single year. These were not just policy changes. These were *life changes*. For our city. For our children.

Between 2011 and 2016, the results were clear: garbage collection decreased by 22%. Recycling rose by 17%. Composting increased by an astounding 221%. And by 2015, Winnipeg's collection was over 230,000 tons of residential waste and recyclables combined. That's not a statistic. In 2015, 59,000 tonnes of recyclable materials only were collected. That's a statement—a loud, clear one that says: *we're capable of doing better when we try*.

But I'd be lying if I said the road has been smooth. There are still potholes—metaphorical and literal—that keep us from becoming the environmental capital we *could* be.

Our recycling system still fails to process many of the items we put into our blue bins. Plastics labelled as recyclable often get sorted out and dumped into landfills due to lack of proper sorting technology. People don't know what goes where. Labels are unclear. Lists are incomplete. And worse—many have given up, believing their efforts don't matter because the system itself is broken.

Let me be clear: *this is unacceptable.*

It is not enough to ask citizens to be responsible—we must also provide them with a system that respects and rewards that responsibility. A system that keeps its promise. If I'm separating my paper, plastics, and organics, I need to know it's being recycled—not dumped in the same place as everything else.

We have the brains. We have the tools. And thanks to companies like **Mother Earth Recycling**, we've seen how this can work. Their Indigenous-led operation has proven that recycling doesn't just help the planet—it creates jobs, builds community, and empowers people with purpose.

Another trailblazer was **Urbanmine**, a company that changed the landscape of scrap metal recycling in 2007. They turned an old industry into a new opportunity, proving that sustainable business is not only possible—but profitable.

And let's not forget the **Omega Garden System**. A rotary hydroponics innovation that I adopted early on—growing vegetables right in my campaign office, even during a Winnipeg winter. Today, we see hydroponics scaling up in places like Churchill, where shipping containers are retrofitted into urban farms. Imagine that—fresh greens in the tundra. *This is the future, friends.*

And still, the city drags its feet.

Why, in 2025, are plastic bags still an issue in some places? Why do we still not have universal compost pickup? Why are there neighbourhoods that feel left behind in the green revolution?

We should be leading the nation—not catching up. Manitoba runs on 95% renewable energy. We have clean hydro, brilliant engineers, passionate residents, and space to grow. We are *uniquely positioned* to be the city that other cities study. The city that didn't wait for federal mandates to do the right thing. The city that dared to be *first.*

And yet, here we are. Still wrestling with the basics.

I say it's time to dream bigger. What if Winnipeg built a world-class facility that integrated waste, recycling, and compost—where garbage entered one end and reusable material, compost, and energy came out the other? What if we turned our landfills into education centres? What if we made zero-waste living *easy*, not exceptional?

These aren't fantasies. They are fully within reach. All it takes is political will and public pressure.

That's why I'm still here. Still speaking. Still marching. Still hoping. Still writing.

Because I believe in this city. I believe in its people. And I believe that if we remember where we came from, we can be very proud of where we're going.

But we must keep going.

Because the job isn't done. Not yet.

Chapter 7

From Policy to Practice — When the Government Finally Moved

For years, I stood on the steps of the Manitoba Legislature, holding up reusable bags, stringing together plastic ones by the tens of thousands, and pleading for a future that didn't bury itself in garbage. I told them that what we called convenience was a slow and silent killer. I told them that if we kept acting like the Earth was disposable, one day we'd realize we had thrown away the only home we've got.

It took time. Too much time, if I'm honest. But eventually, they moved.

After decades of community pressure, scientific warnings, and grassroots momentum, the Government of Manitoba introduced changes to **The Waste Reduction and Prevention Act**, signalling what felt, at least on paper, like a turning point. The bill required the provincial minister to develop a formal plan to reduce the use of single-use plastics. For the first time in the province's legislative history, the words *reduce, reuse,* and *prevent* had legislative teeth behind them.

It wasn't just lip service anymore. There was a date. A commitment.

January 1, 2021—that was the line in the sand. From that day forward, no retailer in Manitoba would be allowed to hand out plastic checkout bags or plastic straws. *Finally.* After years of me walking into stores and being told I was dreaming too big, that plastic bags were "just how it's done," the government had officially caught up to the people.

But the bill didn't stop there.

It laid out an even broader plan—by **January 1, 2025**, the following single-use items would be banned across the province:

- Expanded polystyrene foam containers for food or drink

- Oxo-degradable and oxo-fragmentable plastic products

- Disposable coffee cups

- Plastic water bottles

I read the language twice when it came across my desk. Then a third time, just to make sure I wasn't hallucinating. Manitoba—the same province that once told me to stop wasting council's time—was now banning the very same plastics I had been rallying against since 2007.

It was surreal.

And it wasn't just about what the bill said—it was about what it did. It validated the years of unpaid work, of cold protests, of standing alone in rooms full of skeptical officials. It meant that the *habits* we had spent so long trying to form—bringing reusable bags, refusing plastic straws, questioning the cup we were handed—were no longer fringe behaviour. They were now part of **law.**

Of course, I know that laws alone don't change hearts. But they change behaviours. And over time, behaviour becomes culture.

Today, I see people walking into stores with their own bags—without thinking twice. I see local businesses offering recyclable paper options, compostable takeout containers, and signage that says, "Please help us reduce waste." This isn't performative anymore. It's practice. It's normal.

And it's beautiful.

But just as Manitoba began to find its rhythm, the national picture became more complicated.

Canada had followed suit with the **Single-use Plastics Prohibition Regulations**, announcing a staggered plan to phase out destructive items like plastic cutlery, stir sticks, straws, and ring carriers. It was meant to be a comprehensive federal step forward—ambitious, coordinated, and enforceable.

The federal timelines were clear:

- By **December 20, 2022**, the manufacturing and importation of plastic checkout bags, cutlery, food ware, and more would be prohibited.

- By **December 20, 2023**, the *sale* of those items would stop.

- And by **December 20, 2025**, even exporting them would be banned.

On paper, this was progress. It looked like we were finally turning the corner on decades of environmental damage.

But then came the November 2023 court ruling.

In a blow that many of us feared but few truly anticipated, the **Federal Court retroactively declared** that the government's move to classify "plastic manufactured items" under Schedule 1 of the **Canadian Environmental Protection Act** was *invalid* and *unlawful*. Overnight, what had looked like a national victory was placed on shaky legal ground.

The government, to its credit, didn't fold. They filed an appeal. And by **January 25, 2024**, the Federal Court of Appeal issued a **stay motion**, essentially freezing the lower court's ruling. This meant that the Single-use Plastics Prohibition Regulations could continue—for now.

But the message was loud and clear: *This fight is far from over.*

You see, policy change is one thing. But political will is fragile. One court challenge, one shift in leadership, one lobby group with a well-funded lawyer—and the momentum we spent decades building can be thrown into legal limbo.

That's why I've always said: **we cannot rely solely on governments to lead**. They often follow. What they need—what they *depend on*—is the relentless pressure of people who refuse to let them off the hook like me.

Because when Manitoba acted, it was in no small part because people like me wouldn't stop knocking on their door. When the federal government began banning items one by one, it was because Canadians across the country were already refusing them in their daily lives. The law came after the culture began to change—not before.

So where does that leave us?

It leaves us in a moment of *cautious celebration*. We have made progress. It is real. It is visible. And yet, it is still vulnerable. There are still industries fighting to keep their profits tied to pollution. Still politicians who fear the backlash of making bold environmental decisions. Still citizens who don't understand the cost of doing nothing.

But here's what's also true: we've come too far to go back.

You can't unlearn that a foam container will outlive you by centuries.

You can't unsee the truth that what ends up in our landfills today leeches into our water tomorrow. A dead whale or marine life dead on the beach with their bellies full of plastic, or worse yet, that we are digesting micro-plastics from our seafood.

You can't unknow that 70% of what we used to call trash was recyclable.

We know better now. *So, we must do better.*

I won't stop holding governments to account. Not at the municipal level. Not at the provincial level. And certainly not at the federal level. Because the climate doesn't care about jurisdiction. Pollution doesn't recognize borders. It affects us all—and demands that we rise together.

Let me be clear: this chapter isn't the end of the fight. It's a reminder of what's possible *when people keep pushing.*

It's proof that one man, one voice, one idea—can turn into legislation, regulation, and real-world change.

The bans now in place, the timelines ahead, the new habits forming in homes and businesses across Manitoba and Canada—these are the fruits of long labour. But they are also seeds. Seeds for something bigger. More permanent. More just.

And so, we keep planting.

Because this work isn't about today. It's about tomorrow. It's about the generations who will look back and ask, *"Did they do enough when they still had time?"*

I want to make sure that our answer, however imperfect, will be:

Yes. We started. We are unrelenting and we will never stop.

You will be able to see on the MMSM Simplyrecycle.ca website the following information. They now have a budget through radio & TV ads, print & social media, bus benches, recycling boxes, and billboards that reinforces the importance of recycling. This is very encouraging to see.

Not sure what goes in your recycling bin? Use this poster to help!

ACCEPTED  | UNACCEPTED 

Aluminum and steel containers

Boxboard

Cardboard

Cartons

Glass, clear and coloured

Paper

Plastic packaging*

*Exceptions for plastic packaging: No black plastic, Styrofoam, plastic film

Aluminum foil, pie plates, and trays

Black plastics

Food waste

Healthcare waste

Household hazardous waste containers

Plastic cutlery and plates

Straws

Styrofoam

Textiles

NON-ACCEPTED
MATERIALS

Please do not place any of these items in your blue bins:

Black plastics

Foam packaging of any kind

Aluminum foil, pie plates, and trays

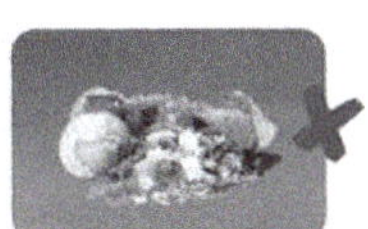
Food waste

Dishes and ceramics

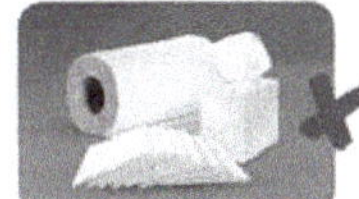
Paper towels, tissues, and napkins

Plastic cutlery

Take out beverage cups

RECYCLING TIPS

Save space in your blue bin by flattening boxes. If your boxes are too large to fit inside your bin, cut them up into smaller pieces.

Toss your recyclables into the bin loosely. Don't stuff containers inside one another. This allows them to be sorted easily at the Material Recovery Facility (MRF).

Ensure your containers and bottles are clean and empty. A quick rinse is always appreciated to get rid of any lingering smells or food residue.

Leave lids and labels on your food and beverage containers.

Don't put anything in your blue bin that your municipality doesn't accept. Check the Recyclepedia at SimplyRecycle.ca or download the free app!

Chapter 8

An Alliance | Major Malls in the city

When you're building a movement—especially one that threatens the comfort and profit margins of powerful players—you quickly realize you need more than conviction. You need allies. And not just any allies, but ones who see beyond the bottom line. Ones who are willing to take a risk. Ones who dare to say, "We'll stand with you."

This chapter is about that kind of courage.

For years, I'd been banging on every media door in the city—radio, television, print—begging someone to take this message seriously. "Let's change the language. Let's change the mindset. Let's call it 'Recycle Day,' not 'Garbage Day.'" But my emails were ignored. My calls unreturned. At one point, I felt like I was just shouting into a void.

Then, a sliver of light broke through that silence. His name was **Matt Cundell,** the program director at **Power 97**. When I first reached out to him, he dismissed me quickly—like so many others. But I kept coming back. I believed that if I could just speak to him—*really* speak to him—I could help him see the vision. I asked for five minutes. That was all.

He finally agreed. With an uninterested look and crossed arms, he sat down at noon. I spoke until 12:05. When I stopped talking, the expression on his face had changed.

"Let's do it," he said.

That meeting turned the tide. Matt didn't just lend me a microphone—he lent me credibility. He started calling it "Recycle Day" on-air. And when Power 97 joined the cause, other media houses slowly followed suit. Suddenly, the word was spreading. The idea was catching fire. *Language,* that once seemed symbolic, became a city-wide statement of intent.

And then, the next level unfolded — *retail.*

Enter **Debra Green,** the General Manager of **Polo Park Shopping Centre**. I will say this without hesitation: Debra was one of the most pivotal people in this movement. She wasn't a politician. She wasn't an environmentalist. But she *was* a leader. And leadership is exactly what she offered when I needed it most.

Debra opened a door I could never have pushed open on my own: a meeting with the executives of the country's largest grocery chains and shopping malls. The big players. The ones with real sway. The meeting wasn't meant for me. I wasn't on the schedule. But Debra made sure I had a voice in that room.

I didn't give a speech. I made a plea.

I told them we didn't need a revolution overnight—just one day. "Give us *one* day," I said. "One day where you don't hand out plastic bags. One day to let the people imagine a better way. Just one day."

And they gave it to us.

March 22, 2010, became **Reusable Bag Day**—a city & nation-wide collaboration where shopping centres, grocery stores, and mall tenants promoted reusable bags instead of plastic ones. Some stores gave them away for free. Others sold them for a token amount. But all of them stood on the same side—for one day.

And that one day changed everything.

Plastic Bag Day at St. Vital Shopping Centre

I'll never forget standing in the middle of Polo Park that morning. The energy was electric. Volunteers lined up, reusable bags in hand. Shoppers arrived curious, skeptical, then inspired. It felt like we weren't just cleaning up a city—we were turning a page in our culture.

I remember children tugging on their parents' sleeves saying, "Can I get one too?" And I remember elderly shoppers saying, "It's about time someone did something like this."

That day showed me the power of collaboration. It proved that when business, media, and citizens come together, we can make the impossible look easy. And it showed me something else: that no movement succeeds without people willing to lend their name, their influence, and sometimes their platform to something greater than themselves.

Because here's the truth: we didn't get a national ban on plastic bags by accident. We got there through days like this—through small moments that grew into national policy.

To see **Walmart** and **Dollarama**—two companies that once depended on plastic bags—now handing out reusable totes… it's surreal.

I still smile every time I see someone carrying a Sobeys bag into No Frills, or a Walmart tote being used at Superstore. We didn't just change shopping habits—we sparked *unintentional cross-marketing*. That's the kind of cultural shift most corporations dream of. And we did it by pushing for one, simple act of responsibility.

This was never about perfection. It was about participation. And the day the malls got on board was the day the tide truly turned.

I want to thank **Kildonan Place, St. Vital Shopping Centre**, and **Sobeys,** who all joined Polo Park in making Reusable Bag Day such a success. Some gave away branded totes. Others educated customers. All of them became allies in the mission. And it mattered.

Don presenting a passenger's reusable bag that identifies as a suitcase.

When I say I'm grateful, I don't mean that lightly. I mean it with the full weight of every rejection, every slammed door, every moment when I thought maybe no one would ever care.

Because here's what I know now: *enough people do care.*

And sometimes, all it takes is one bold "yes" to move an entire city forward.

So, to everyone who took that chance with me—thank you. You proved that when hearts align and hands unite, we can leave this planet better than we found it.

And to those still wondering if their voice matters: *look around.* It's working. The tide has already begun to turn.

Chapter 9

The impacts of a mother who volunteered

Before I was a community leader, a filmmaker, or an environmental activist, I was simply the son of a woman who gave everything she had to others—and then asked if she could give more.

My mother, **Dothlyn Woodstock**, was the first person to show me what true service looks like. We attended **Boulevard Baptist Church** in Kingston, Jamaica, and if there was a sign-up sheet for volunteers, she was the first one to scribble her name. Food drives, clothing collections, school fundraisers, church banquets—you name it, she was there. But she wasn't just "there." She was *present*—heart, mind, and spirit.

Growing up, I used to think she had some kind of secret energy reserve. She would teach all day in school, come home, cook dinner for the family, and still find the strength to organize a bake sale for the church or run off to help a neighbour in need. And there I was—usually right behind her—carrying a folding chair or handing out juice boxes to kids who didn't have much. She didn't ask me if I wanted to help. She showed me *how* to help. And I followed her lead because, deep down, I understood *this is how you build community*.

Towards the end of her life, my mother was honoured by the **Government of Jamaica** for her dedication and long career in education. It was one of the proudest moments of my life. To see her receive that recognition wasn't just gratifying—it was affirming. It affirmed that a life of service is never wasted. That the seeds she planted—through her students, her church, and her family—had grown into trees that would bear fruit for years to come.

She wasn't a woman of many jokes, but she had a warmth and generosity that made everyone around her feel safe. If you came to our house, she'd give you the last dumpling from the pot and then ask if you were full. She had so little and gave so much. She lived her life as if kindness was currency and love, was an unlimited resource.

It's because of her that I chose this path. Every petition I've started, every door I've knocked on, every banner I've held—was rooted in the example she gave me. And as I lobbied for the name change from

Garbage Day to Recycle Day, as I fought for environmental equity and awareness in every corner of Winnipeg, I carried her spirit with me.

I didn't realize it at first, but I was repeating her rhythm: *see a need, fill it. See a void, step into it.* Be the first to volunteer, even if you're the only one. Because someone must be the first spark before the fire catches.

That's why, when I had the chance to volunteer as **Phil the Blue Box**, the city's recycling mascot, I jumped at it. Some people laughed at me. Others said I was wasting my time. But I knew that the real power of change begins in the hearts of children. If I could make recycling fun—if I could get a smile out of a seven-year-old while handing them a blue bin sticker—then maybe, just maybe, I could help create new habits that would last a lifetime.

Having fun at the Festival du Voyageur with other mascots — Goldie from the Goldeyes, Sparky from the Police and others.

Don putting on his Phil the Blue Box mascot costume.

I wore that foam mascot suit at malls, at community events, at outdoor festivals, and even at **Festival du Voyageur**. I may have only known how to say "Bonjour," but I didn't need to speak French to connect with those kids. I danced. I waved. I pointed to bins and acted out sorting routines. I became a walking, smiling embodiment of my mother's values: serve without ego, and love without limits.

And then there were the races. One of my favourite memories as Phil was competing at **Assiniboine Downs Racetrack** against other mascots like Buzz and Boomer of the Winnipeg Blue Bombers and "Copper," the police service mascot. Let's just say I didn't win. Buzz cut me off, and I almost demanded a steward's inquiry! But we all laughed, we all bonded, and in that silliness, I saw the seriousness of what we were doing. We were planting ideas in young minds that would outlive our slogans and banners.

Eventually, the city decided to retire Phil the Blue Box. It broke my heart a little. I had advocated for giving the new blue carts a personality—something fun and friendly that would keep the momentum going. But others couldn't see the vision. They thought it was time to move on.

Even so, I look back on those four years with a deep sense of fulfilment. Because when you believe in something, you *live* it. You embody it. You wear the costume, you show up when nobody else will, you smile even when they mock you. You do the job that needs doing— even if it means sweating in a mascot suit while racing down a track for a cause you believe in.

That's what my mother taught me.

And so, to **Dothlyn Woodstock**, I say this: thank you. Thank you for giving me the blueprint. Thank you for teaching me that service isn't about spotlight—it's about impact. Thank you for showing me that when you give selflessly, you never really lose anything. You gain a life filled with meaning.

Rest well, Mom. Your work continues—in me, in my children, and in every recycled can, every composted leaf, and every young mind inspired to protect this Earth.

Because of you, I learned that volunteering isn't just about helping. It's about *healing*. It's about *hope*. And it's about *leaving behind a legacy that will never decompose.*

Left to right: Kaedon Woodstock (Don's son), Dothlyn and Don at the Baptist Boulevard Church in Kingston, Jamaica.

Chapter 10

Turning your negatives into positive action

I've often said that rejection is not the end of the road. It's a detour. It's the universe whispering, "Not this door, not yet—but keep walking." And if you walk long enough, with your head held high and your purpose intact, you'll eventually find a door that doesn't just open—it swings wide.

But I won't sugar-coat it. My journey as an activist, as a Black man with a strong Jamaican accent in a city that wasn't always ready for either, has been brutal at times. Winnipeg has given me some of the most beautiful moments of my life—but it has also given me some of the ugliest.

When I began my push for environmental reform—plastic bag bans, recycling initiatives, educational media—I wasn't met with applause. I was met with silence. And when the silence broke, it came in the form of insults. People questioned my credibility. They questioned my identity. "What are you doing here?" "You think this city will listen to someone like you?" "Go back to your country."

That last one hit me hard. Because Canada *is* my country. I chose it. I've paid taxes here. I've voted here. I've raised my children here. I've fought to make this place cleaner, kinder, better. And yet, time and again, I was reminded that for some, no amount of contribution could ever outweigh the colour of my skin or the accent in my voice.

But I refused to let hate to shrink my purpose.

I'd heard "no" so many times, it started to sound like background noise. But I kept showing up. Because deep down, I knew this was never about winning popularity contests—it was about planting roots deep enough to survive any storm.

I'll never forget visiting a media house on St. Anne's Road, determined to pitch a public service campaign about Recycle Day. I walked in with optimism and left with shame. The looks. The smirks. The condescension. One person flat out told me, "Nobody's going to care about what you're saying. We've got bigger things to worry about than garbage."

I walked out into the Winnipeg cold, pulled my coat tighter, and whispered, "We'll see."

That became my battle cry: *We'll see.*

I didn't just go back to my drawing board—I went back to my roots. I thought of my grandfather sending me to the river with a basket. I thought of my mother, volunteering at the church with a smile even after a long day of work. I thought of all the people who had been told they didn't belong, and yet still built empires from ashes.

And then, being unrelentless I got back to work.

The negativity didn't stop. I visited another media house on Osborne Street, and again, I was met with derision. One of them said—without a hint of irony— "Aren't Black people supposed to be worried about crime or poverty? Why are *you* talking about plastic bags?"

It took everything in me not to respond with anger. But I didn't let them see my frustration. Instead, I smiled. Because I knew something they didn't: *they were already losing*. Every time they dismissed me, someone else picked up a reusable bag. Every insult was another reason to keep going. Every rejection was a reminder of why this unrelenting pursuit mattered.

Eventually, my persistence cracked through the noise. The same media houses that ignored me started calling me back. The same people who once laughed at "Recycle Day" started using the term on air. The change was slow, but it was undeniable.

You see, turning your negatives into positive action isn't just about staying strong. It's about *redirecting your energy*. It's about transforming pain into purpose. I didn't let the slurs break me. I used them to dig deeper. I let them fuel the fire that kept me walking into rooms where I wasn't invited—until the rooms started to change.

I believe rejection is divine redirection. Because if everyone had said yes from the beginning, I never would've learned to fight this hard. And if I hadn't fought this hard, I wouldn't have discovered just how much strength was living inside me.

It's like owning your first puppy. You think it'll be all playtime and tail wags. But then the dog chews your shoes, has accidents in the house, and demands your energy at every hour of the night. Still, something amazing happens. You grow attached. You learn to care more than you thought you could. And suddenly, this labour becomes a joy. A responsibility you're proud to carry.

That's what this journey has been for me. Difficult, messy, and sometimes unfair. But also rewarding beyond words.

So, to the people who told me to stop 'I *thank you*'. To the ones who said I couldn't: '*watch me*'. You thought your negativity would bury me. But all you did was teach me how to grow like a flower that grows & blooms in the crack of the concrete.

And to anyone out there facing rejection right now—whether because of your race, your gender, your ideas, or your accent—I want you to know this:

Keep walking.

The road might be lonely. The voices might be cruel. But the work you are doing—the purpose you carry—is bigger than the pain you're facing.

Don't quit. Don't shrink. Don't apologize for the fire in your heart.

Because sometimes, the people who told you "No" the loudest will one day tell their children, "I remember when I met that person… before the world caught up to them."

And when that day comes, you'll smile—not out of spite, but out of satisfaction.

Because you turned your negatives into action. And in doing so, you changed the world.

"Quitters never win, and Winners never quit!"

Chapter 11

The Electrification of buses in Winnipeg

There's a moment in every advocate's life when you realize that your fight isn't just about fixing what's broken—it's about waking people up to what's possible. I had that moment the day I stood at a Winnipeg Transit bus stop, inhaling the thick diesel exhaust of an idling bus, watching young children nearby cover their mouths as they waited to board. Something about that image—a simple, everyday scene—hit me like a punch to the chest.

We were poisoning our own future, one breath at a time.

As an environmentalist and as a human being, I couldn't accept that. Especially not in a city that had two of the greatest assets in all of Canada for sustainable public transportation: **Manitoba Hydro** and **New Flyer Industries**. One provides nearly 100% renewable hydroelectric energy, and the other builds world-class **electric buses**, right here in our own backyard.

I kept asking myself: *How is this not already happening?* How are we still running dirty diesel buses through residential neighbourhoods, polluting the air, contributing to the degradation of our climate, and paying for fuel we don't even need—when the solution is staring us in the face?

It made no sense. So, I decided to make noise.

At the time, I was working at **Winnipeg Transit** as a bus operator. I've always believed in working from within the system while simultaneously challenging it. Driving those buses gave me a front-row seat to the flaws and frustrations that riders and operators face every day. It also made the disconnect even more glaring: Why are we using fossil fuels when we literally have a bus manufacturer and renewable power in our own province?

That's when I approached **Jim Rondeau**, the then-Minister of Industry, Trade and Commerce. I brought a simple, bold proposal: *We need to electrify Winnipeg's transit fleet.* Not tomorrow. *Now.*

I wasn't coming to him with a dream—I was coming with a plan. Electric buses were already in production. The charging infrastructure could be scaled. Hydro had the capacity. The environmental benefits were proven. The economic benefits were undeniable—less maintenance, fewer emissions, lower fuel costs, and jobs created right here in Manitoba.

*In 2015, Don standing beside the first
Winnipeg 'Electric Transit Bus'.*

But like many of my proposals, this too was met with the usual skepticism. I was "too passionate," "too idealistic," "too impatient." But here's the thing: if you've ever stood in a diesel-filled transit garage, if you've ever seen the black soot clinging to the sides of a bus depot, if you've ever looked a child in the eyes and realized they're breathing that in—you'll understand why *patience* was a luxury I couldn't afford.

We don't have time to wait for perfect conditions. The climate crisis doesn't care about bureaucracy. Every day we delay is a day we trade clean air for toxic fumes. And that's not just an environmental issue—it's a public health emergency.

But I didn't just talk the talk. I lived it.

In 2022, I made a personal decision that further aligned my life with my values. I purchased a **Ford Mustang Mach-E**, a fully electric vehicle. It wasn't just about reducing my carbon footprint—it was a public declaration that *the future is here*, and it's time for us to catch up. I plugged it in, drove silently through the streets, and imagined a city where every bus, every service vehicle, every delivery van did the same.

Don purchased a 2021 Ford Mustang Mach E — all electric. 0-60kms in 2.6 seconds. Wow!

I'm dreaming of a Winnipeg where the only sound you hear on transit routes is the quiet hum of progress.

And the best part? That dream is completely achievable.

We've already seen great strides. **Manitoba Hydro's Great Falls Generating Station** alone produces 130 megawatts of renewable energy. Our province is blessed with an abundance of clean power. Our people are ready. Our workers are capable. The only thing missing is consistent political will.

And don't let anyone tell you it's too expensive. In the long run, electric transit is cheaper, more reliable, and far healthier for our city. The upfront cost is an investment—not an expense. It's an investment in cleaner air, lower emissions, and jobs in green manufacturing.

New Flyer, headquartered right here, is leading the charge across North America. Cities across the continent are electrifying their fleets—with buses *built in Winnipeg*. Imagine that: buses made here, used everywhere—*except here.*

We are standing at the intersection of innovation and inertia. The future is waving at us from across the street, and yet our feet are frozen. We need leadership that doesn't just look at spreadsheets but looks at children coughing in traffic. We need policies that are bold, unapologetic, and rooted in the long-term health of our city.

I believe Winnipeg has what it takes to become a global model for clean transportation. Not just because we *should*, but because we *can*. We are geographically cantered, logistically sound, and environmentally blessed. With the right infrastructure, we could connect communities, reduce emissions, and show the rest of Canada what commitment to climate justice looks like.

But we must act. And we must act with courage.

When I think about the future of Winnipeg, I don't just see policies—I see *people*. I see children breathing easier. I see seniors boarding buses that glide instead of growl. I see drivers taking pride in operating vehicles that honour the earth. I see a city that doesn't wait for permission to do the right thing—it *leads*.

To those who think change is too hard, too expensive, or too ambitious, I say: look at what we've already done. Look at Recycle Day. Look at reusable bags. Look at hydroponic food systems in shipping containers. Look at every battle we've fought—and won.

If we could do all that starting from nothing, imagine what we could do now.

The electrification of buses is not a fantasy. It's not a maybe. It's not a someday. It is a **necessity**. And it's *doable*. We have the pieces. It's time to put the puzzle together.

Because the question isn't whether we can afford to transition to electric buses.

The question is: *can we afford not to?*

Chapter 12

The Day – September 12, 2009

There are moments in life that don't just mark time—they make history. For me, **September 12, 2009**, was one of those days. Not because I received an award or landed a high-profile interview, but because I watched a city rise. Because I witnessed, with my own eyes, what happens when people come together—not for profit, not for fame, but for purpose.

We called it **International Day to Ban Plastic Bags**. But for those of us on the frontlines, it was more than just a campaign or a one-day event—it was a breakthrough.

The morning began with sunshine and the buzz of preparation. The temperature hovered around 20 degrees Celsius, a perfect fall day in Winnipeg. But it wasn't the weather that made it magical—it was the spirit. There was excitement in the air, a kind of quiet momentum. We didn't know what to expect. Would people show up? Would they understand what we were trying to do?

And then—*they came.*

Like a wave cresting, people began pouring into the **Legislative Grounds**. At first, it was a few families, some children with curious eyes, shoppers carrying their stashes of plastic bags, unsure if they were in the right place. But by mid-morning, it was a *flood*. Young people, seniors, students, parents, local business owners—all carrying bundles of plastic bags they were ready to surrender for something better. A change. A statement.

Sobeys, led by Mike Lupien, was on-site with thousands of reusable bags. We had no idea how we were going to give them all away. Would people take them? Would we have extras? But those bags flew out of our hands like gifts on Christmas morning.

Kathy Harris, a representative from Sobey's and Kathy's sister, Bonnie Dumontier

By noon, it was clear—this day had become bigger than us.

The energy was electric. There was music. There were speeches. But the real showstopper was the **plastic bag chain**. We strung together bags donated by Winnipeggers—tattered, torn, clean, dirty, faded by use. These were bags that had been hiding under kitchen sinks, stuffed in drawers, blowing in alleyways, polluting rivers. And now, we turned them into a symbol.

The chain stretched around the **Legislative Grounds not once— but twice**. We wrapped it around like a scarf of shame and transformation. Almost like decorating the trees with Christmas lights. The grounds were filled from end-to-end with plastic bags. People stopped in their tracks. Some cried. Some just stared. One woman turned to me and said, "I had no idea it was this bad."

63

That's what the day was about: *waking people up*.

We weren't here to make anyone feel guilty. We were here to remind them that small choices add up—and that those choices can either poison our future or protect it. We collected over **44,000 plastic bags** that day. *Forty-four thousand*. That's not just a number—it's a movement. And it happened in a single day.

We gave away **over 4,000 reusable bags** in exchange. But what we really gave away was a new way of thinking. We gave people a chance to look at the world differently. To see that sustainability isn't some faraway dream—it's something we can hold in our hands. Quite literally.

And the media came. Thanks to **Matt Cundell** at **Power 97** and **Kick FM**, and **ChrisD, Winnipeg's** top local media influencer & photographer, word had gotten out. For the first time, the cameras pointed at *us*—at the people, not the politicians. At the change, not the chaos.

There's a picture burned into my memory—one of **fifteen tally sheets**, hand-written, ink smudged from the rush of the day, each tracking thousands of bags turned in. We had planned, organized, sweated, and prayed. But nothing could have prepared me for the overwhelming pride I felt when I saw those sheets.

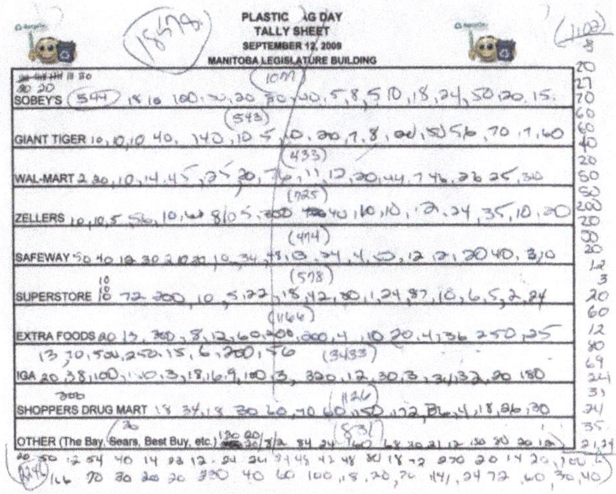

Winnipeggers had shown up.

They had stood tall. Not for me, but for *us*—for the Earth, for their children, for the belief that we could do better.

To those who joined me that day, I say thank you. You proved that civic engagement isn't dead. You proved that caring about the environment doesn't belong to one party or one class or one community. It belongs to all of us.

And to those who said it couldn't be done—to those who said nobody would come, that plastic bags didn't matter, that the city didn't care—I offer a gentle, defiant smile.

Because we did it.

We turned awareness into action. We took a stand in a way that could not be ignored. That day became the catalyst for more national conversations. That day helped lay the groundwork for Canada's eventual ban on single-use plastic bags. That day proved that *one voice*—when joined by many—can echo through history.

So, if you ever wonder whether your presence matters, whether your choice to bring a reusable bag makes a difference, whether showing up for one day changes anything—remember September 12, 2009.

It started with a few people and a dream.

And it ended with a movement.

Chapter 13

Where We Are Today / And Tomorrow

Let's talk about progress. Real progress. The kind that doesn't just show up in pie charts and policy papers but changes the way people live, think, and act. Because that's the only kind of progress I've ever cared about—the kind that leaves a mark not on headlines, but on hearts.

Today, we are not where we started. Not even close.

Fifteen years ago, plastic bags were handed out like candy at every store. You'd walk into a grocery store, buy a loaf of bread, and leave with three bags. No questions asked. No second thoughts. The environment? Not even part of the conversation. We were trapped in a culture of convenience, and convenience was killing our planet.

But we've come a long way since then.

Take the simple act of grocery shopping. It used to be normal to come home with 25 plastic bags per trip—some doubled up for heavy items. Do that three times a month, twelve months a year, and you're looking at *900 plastic bags* stuffed under your sink by the end of the year. Multiply that by every household in a city like Winnipeg and you begin to understand the scale of the problem. Now, think about the fact that plastic can take *50 years or more* to decompose—leaching toxins into our waterways, harming wildlife, and poisoning the earth in the process.

That was the norm. That was accepted.

But not anymore.

Today, we see reusable bags everywhere—Sobeys, Walmart, Superstore, No Frills. It's not just a new habit. It's a *new culture*. And it's powerful. People are choosing reusable not because they're forced to, but because they finally understand the *why*. And that's the greatest victory of all—when you change the mind, the behaviour follows.

And let's not overlook the irony: reusable bags from Walmart being carried into Canadian Tire, Shopper's Drug Mart bags spotted at No Frills. This unintentional cross-marketing is a thing of beauty. A dream, really. Stores are promoting their brands in the aisles of competitors, not through flashy ads, but through the quiet revolution of everyday people choosing sustainability.

That's what I call poetic justice.

We didn't just stop plastic bags. We started something bigger. A mindset shift. A new normal. And I see it everywhere now. In the faces of young people leading climate marches. In the grandparents bringing cloth bags to the market. In the schools organizing composting programs. In the neighbourhoods pushing for greener spaces.

But let's not get too comfortable. Because while we've made tremendous strides, the work is far from done.

Yes, we've reduced our plastic bag use. Yes, we've improved recycling participation. Yes, we've normalized reusable culture. But there are still glaring gaps, especially in our infrastructure. Many items that carry the recycling symbol can't be processed by Winnipeg's current facilities. People diligently sort their waste, only for it to end up in the landfill anyway.

That's more than frustrating. That's betrayal.

If we ask people to care, we owe them a system that honours their effort. If someone rinses their containers, separates their waste, and drags their blue bin to the curb every week, they deserve to know that what they're doing *matters*. And right now, too often, it doesn't.

That's not just inefficient. That's dangerous. Because when people lose faith in the process, they disengage. And disengagement is the death of change.

So where do we go from here?

We go *bigger*. We go *bolder*. We stop thinking in terms of small tweaks and start thinking in terms of *transformation*. We need recycling facilities that are as advanced as our ideals. We need sorting systems that match the commitment of our citizens. We need education campaigns that reach every classroom, every neighbourhood, every demographic. We need composting programs city-wide—not as a luxury, but as a standard.

And more than anything, we need to build what I've dreamed about for years: an *integrated environmental processing facility*—a place where garbage, compost, and recycling all enter through one side and are sorted, processed, and reborn on the other. A facility that turns waste into opportunity. A model that other cities can copy.

Because that's what Winnipeg should be—a leader. Not just in rhetoric, but in *results*.

The truth is the next chapter of this story will be written by all of us. Governments, businesses, communities, and everyday citizens. This can't be the mission of a few anymore—it must be the movement of the many.

So, I leave you with this:

When you carry your reusable bag, when you separate your recyclables, when you vote for leaders who care about the planet—*you are part of the solution*. You are honouring the work of generations before you and building something better for the ones to come.

And if anyone ever tells you that one person can't make a difference, tell them about Winnipeg. Tell them about a city that stood up. Tell them about September 12, 2009. Tell them about Recycle Day. Tell them about a man who carried water in a basket until it overflowed with hope.

Because today, we're not just saving the planet.

We're redefining what it means to *care*.

And tomorrow? Tomorrow belongs to those who believe that what we do today—*right now*—can still change the world.

Chapter 14

When the Youth Take the Torch

If there's one truth that has been confirmed for me time and time again, it's this: real change doesn't end with us—it begins with those who come after. And today, I can say with pride and certainty that the youth are not only ready to take the torch—they've already lit their own fires.

Throughout my journey, I've spoken to countless students—from kindergarteners with hands sticky from finger paint to teenagers burning with questions bigger than most adults are willing to answer. I've walked into school gyms, community centres, after-school clubs, and classrooms packed with the future of our city—curious, bright-eyed, and already asking the kind of questions that push society forward. And each time I leave one of those spaces, I walk away feeling hopeful, energized, and deeply humbled.

Because they *get it*. They get it in ways many adults still don't.

These young people are growing up in a world we helped create. They see the plastic swirling in our rivers. They feel the heatwaves growing stronger each summer. They scroll through news feeds filled with wildfires, floods, and melting ice caps. They know—*deeply know*—that they are inheriting a planet on the edge.

But instead of running from that truth, they run *toward* it.

They speak out. They organize. They invent. They *show up*.

And every time I witness that, I feel a deep sense of responsibility—not to lead forever, but to step aside when the time is right and cheer them on from the sidelines. Because the role of any good changemaker is not to hog the stage, but to build the platform and hand over the microphone.

I remember walking into a school just outside downtown Winnipeg. It was a rainy day—typical for spring. The staff had invited me to talk about recycling and environmental responsibility. I prepared a short talk. Nothing flashy. But before I could even open my mouth, a Grade 3 student stood up and asked, "Mr. Woodstock, why does the city still use garbage trucks if most of it could be recycled or composted?"

Now, tell me that isn't the future speaking truth to power.

I smiled. Because in that moment, I saw myself in him—someone unwilling to accept "that's just the way it is" as an answer.

Over the years, I've heard hundreds of stories from students and youth organizers who were touched by the work we did—by *Recycle Day*, by *Reusable Bag Day*, by my time as Phil the Blue Box, or even from watching an episode of *U, Me and the Environment*. They took those seeds, planted them in their schools, homes, and neighbourhoods, and nurtured something new. Compost programs. Clean-up drives. Letter-writing campaigns to City Hall. Social media activism. Eco clubs raising awareness and raising hell.

One young woman wrote me after attending an Earth Day rally. She said, "I didn't know people like me could change anything until I saw someone like you doing it first."

That message stuck with me.

Because that's the legacy we're building—not one of perfection, but of permission. When young people see you trying, failing, pushing, and persisting, it tells them they *can too*. You don't have to be rich. You don't have to be famous. You just must care enough to act.

And act, they have.

I've watched middle-schoolers challenge their school boards to eliminate single-use plastics. I've seen high schoolers build compost bins from scratch using repurposed wood and start small gardens in school courtyards. I've seen university students launch full-blown campaigns demanding climate action from city councillors. They don't wait. They do.

They are proof that all the early mornings, all the doors slammed in my face, all the emails ignored, all the racist slurs I endured—*they were never in vain* because these were young people taking action. They were listening. Even when it seemed like nobody else was.

And that's why we keep going.

Because someone out there is watching us. Learning from us. Planning to do better because *they saw us try*.

To Aspyn and Julian—my babies, now growing into leaders in their own right—I see you. I hear you. And I trust you. Your questions, your passion, your refusal to accept mediocrity reminds me daily that this work doesn't end with me. It lives on in you.

To every child who's ever pointed out a piece of litter and picked it up... To every teen who decided to carry a reusable water bottle to school... To every college student who started their own green business... You are the torchbearers.

Take it.

Carry it with pride.

But carry it with courage too. Because there will be days when people tell you to sit down, be quiet, follow the rules. There will be days when your voice shakes, when your vision feels too big, when your efforts feel too small. But don't stop. Don't dim. Don't wait for approval.

You are the ones we've been waiting for.

So light up your schools, your cities, your communities, and this entire country with your passion, your ideas, and your unshakable hope.

The world is watching.

And now—*it's your turn.*

Chapter 15

Seeds in the Snow – Urban Farming for the Future

When people think of Winnipeg, they often picture bitter winds, snowdrifts the size of small cars, and a winter season that seems to last from Halloween to Easter. And to be fair, they're not wrong. This is one of the coldest major cities on Earth. But while many see that as a limitation, I've always seen it as a challenge—a dare, even.

Can you grow life where nothing should grow?

I say yes.

That's the mindset that led me into the world of **urban farming** and **hydroponics**—the belief that nature doesn't quit in the cold, and neither should we. And when you look past the frostbitten fingertips and frozen sidewalks, you start to see something else: *potential*. Winnipeg might be cold, but it's not barren. It's a blank canvas. And I was determined to paint it green.

My first real foray into indoor growing came from pure necessity. I was frustrated with the seasonal limitations, the rising price of produce, and the carbon footprint of trucking food into a province that's rich in water, light, and innovation. I began researching **rotary hydroponics systems**, and that's when I discovered the **Omega Garden**—a brilliant Canadian invention designed to grow food in controlled environments, all year round, using minimal water and space.

And just like that, the idea was planted: *what if we could grow fresh, healthy vegetables indoors, in the middle of a Winnipeg winter?*

So I rolled up my sleeves—literally—and got to work.

I set up my first Omega Garden system in a small room. No giant warehouse. No massive staff. Just me, a drum-shaped rotating garden, some LED lights, and a whole lot of enthusiasm. Within weeks, leafy greens began to sprout. Spinach, lettuce, basil—vibrant, alive, untouched by snow or smog.

I was growing food while snow pounded the streets outside.

People thought I was crazy—until they saw it for themselves. I brought this system into my **campaign office during the 2015 election**. Right there, among signs and flyers, grew living proof that sustainability isn't just a slogan—it's a practice. Visitors would walk in, stunned to see tomatoes ripening next to political posters. That was the point. *Change doesn't wait for perfect conditions. It grows wherever we make room for it.*

And we're not talking about some abstract, far-off dream. Hydroponics is already reshaping how cities think about food. Look at **Churchill, Manitoba**, where a retrofitted shipping container now grows leafy vegetables year-round using hydroponic technology. They've literally turned frozen tundra into farmland. If Churchill can do it—if *I* can do it in a converted office—what's stopping the rest of us?

This is what I call planting **seeds in the snow**.

It's not just a metaphor for growing vegetables—it's a philosophy for life. It's the belief that innovation can take root anywhere, even in the most unlikely environments. That we don't need to wait for spring or permission or perfect timing to begin transforming our world.

Winnipeg has every resource to become a hub of green innovation. We have space. We have light. We have water. And most importantly, we have *need*. Food insecurity is rising. Climate change is disrupting global agriculture. And the farther our food travels, the more it costs us—not just financially, but environmentally.

Urban farming offers a solution that's local, sustainable, and empowering. It reconnects people to the earth, even when the ground outside is frozen. It gives communities control over their food. It creates jobs, teaches skills, and reduces our dependence on fossil-fuelled supply chains.

But like anything worth doing, it requires vision—and willpower.

We need to invest in indoor farming infrastructure. We need to support entrepreneurs who want to turn warehouses into vertical farms. We need to introduce hydroponics in schools, teaching kids that agriculture doesn't just belong in rural fields—it belongs in cities, rooftops, basements, and balconies.

Imagine a Winnipeg where community centres grow their own greens. Where seniors' homes have rotating garden walls that provide fresh produce. Where local restaurants pick their ingredients from down the hall instead of halfway across the continent. It's possible. It's happening elsewhere. Why not here?

I'm not suggesting that hydroponics will replace traditional farming. But it can *complement* it. It can bridge gaps. It can bring food sovereignty to communities that have been shut out for too long. It can make resilience a way of life—not just a buzzword.

So yes, I've grown lettuce next to political literature. I've watched basil flourish under fluorescent lights. And each time I harvest a crop in January, I'm reminded of something essential: **we are only limited by the size of our imagination**.

Seeds in the snow don't just grow plants.

They grow possibility.

They remind us that the harshest climates—whether of weather, politics, or poverty—are no match for human creativity.

And if Winnipeg dares to believe that we can grow something far greater than vegetables.

We can grow a *future*.

Chapter 16

From One Voice to Many – Building a
Coalition for the Earth

There was a time—not so long ago—when I believed that passion alone could change the world. I believed that if I shouted loud enough, marched hard enough, or sacrificed long enough, that the system would wake up. That the people with power would listen. And for a time, that belief kept me alive.

But belief, like breath, needs others to sustain it.

And what I came to realize—painfully, humbly—is that change doesn't happen because one voice screams into the dark. It happens because that voice is heard, echoed, and eventually *amplified* by others.

In the early days of my work, I didn't know what the word "coalition" really meant. I thought it meant formal meetings, handshakes, maybe a few letters of support from organizations with long acronyms. But coalition isn't a banner you hang over a table.

It's a relationship. A living, breathing, evolving thing.

It's when a custodian in a downtown school offers to save paper towel tubes so the students can build a sculpture about waste. It's when a bus driver tells me he changed his route to stop at the recycling depot on his lunch break. It's when a teenager creates a TikTok video about composting and it gets more views than any press releases I've ever written.

Those are my people.

Those are my coalition.

The beauty of a coalition is that it begins with just one act of trust. One moment where someone decides to believe in the work not because it's trending, but because it feels *true*. I can still remember the day I sat in a dimly lit church basement beside an elder who barely said a word. We were there to talk about a proposed green initiative. Everyone else had their laptops open, their data slides ready. And she just sat, quietly knitting. When the meeting ended, she handed me a small note. On it, she had written: "Plant seeds. Not just in the earth. But in people."

That line has never left me.

And that's what building a coalition has become for me—not strategy, but *sowing*. Planting seeds in people's lives. Not just with statistics or programs, but with moments. With stories. With invitations to take one small step toward a shared future.

I've built relationships with people I never expected to. A former city engineer who volunteers weekends teaching kids how to build solar ovens from cardboard and tinfoil. A barbershop owner who put out a recycling bin and now runs a clean-up crew every second Sunday in his neighbourhood—just because he "couldn't unsee" what he saw in one of my talks.

We didn't meet at a press conference. We didn't draft a memo. We crossed paths because we cared. And that care became connection. That connection became collaboration.

And here's the truth no one tells you about building a movement: the people who change the world rarely do it full-time. They do it in between shifts. In grocery lines. On coffee breaks. In the carpool lane. They do it not for applause or political capital, but because *something inside them refuses to be quiet.*

This chapter of my life—the coalition-building chapter—has been less about being out front and more about walking beside. Listening more than speaking. Encouraging more than directing. Watching people take ownership of the message in ways I never could have imagined.

One of the most powerful moments of this journey came not from a public event or a campaign milestone, but in a dim garage behind a youth drop-in centre. A group of young men had decided to repurpose old skateboards into portable planters for herbs. They were caked in sawdust, hands full of splinters, laughing their heads off. One of them said, "We thought this environmental stuff was for other people. But now it's just what we do."

And that's when I knew: the torch was already being passed. Not with speeches. With *action*. With culture. With camaraderie.

This movement has never been about making everyone care about *everything*. It's been about finding out what each person already cares about—and helping them protect it in a way that also protects the Earth.

That's the genius of coalition. It meets people where they are. It speaks their language. It makes room for difference and builds strength from it.

I no longer feel like I'm walking alone. Not because the crowd suddenly showed up, but because I stopped needing the crowd to prove my worth.

I've built something better.

A web. A community. A coalition not built on uniformity, but on *shared responsibility.*

From one voice to many, we have become a force. Not because we always agree, but because we're always aligned on one thing: this planet matters. And so do the people on it.

So, if you're out there trying to build your own movement, let me offer you this:

Start small. Start soft. Start human.

Because you never know when your quietest ally may become your loudest amplifier.

And the day you stop fighting alone, you'll realize *you were never alone to begin with.*

Chapter 17

Winning the Long Game

Meaningful journeys demand time. Not just hours or days, but *years*—sometimes *decades*. You don't win the kind of fight I've been in with a single policy change, or by going viral, or by getting a pat on the back from someone in office. The real battles—the ones that matter most—aren't measured in moments. They're measured in **grit**.

I've spent over two decades advocating for something as basic and essential as environmental responsibility. Something as obvious as recycling. As logical as banning plastic bags. As human as wanting cleaner air and greener communities for our children. And yet, I was made to feel like I was asking for the moon.

Let me tell you, being unrelenting in the face of constant resistance takes more than passion—it takes **stamina of spirit and faith in God.**

The truth is, not everyone will clap when you take a stand. In fact, most won't. Some will resist you because they profit from the way things are. Others will reject you simply because you don't look or sound like what they're used to. I've had city officials roll their eyes and even get up & leave the room as I spoke. I've had radio stations hang up on me, tell me never to come back to their office. I've been called an outsider, a troublemaker, and sometimes worse.

But I learned early: if you only speak up when it's easy, you'll never be heard when it really matters.

People talk about "the long game" like it's a strategy. For me, it's been a lifestyle. I've had to dig deep through every delay, every laugh behind closed doors, every time someone dismissed my idea only to repackage it later as their own. I've had to learn how to be patient, how to pivot, how to speak truth when no one is listening—*and keep speaking until they do.*

There were times when it felt like I was pushing a boulder uphill alone. But what kept me going wasn't the hope of recognition. It was the unshakable belief that *somebody had to care enough to keep pushing.*

And so, I did.

Because I've never been afraid of slow progress. What I fear is apathy. I fear the comfort that leads to complacency. The shrug. The sigh. The quiet acceptance of pollution and waste as the price of modern life.

But here's what I know now: every fight I chose, every meeting I attended where I was last on the list, every news outlet that ignored my emails, every political door that was shut in my face—*they all taught me something.* Not just about the system, but about myself.

I learned that change doesn't happen because people agree with you—it happens because you *refuse to leave the room.* You stay long enough that they can't pretend you're not there. You show up again and again until your presence becomes the norm, and your ideas are suddenly "worth considering."

I didn't get here by luck. I got here by **wearing them down** with consistency. One step at a time. One phone call. One press release. One school visit. One protest. One policy pitch. One street corner with a clipboard and a vision. Being unrelenting.

This is what commitment looks like when it's tested.

There were victories—yes. But the real success isn't in the headlines. It's in the **mindset shift** I've seen take hold. People now pause before tossing something in the trash. They ask questions about where their waste goes. They bring their reusable bags with pride. They talk to their kids about composting. And they look around, even in this cold prairie city, and wonder: *How can I do more?*

That's the win. That's what the long game earns you—not just temporary compliance, but *permanent cultural change.*

But don't be fooled—there's still plenty of work to do. Our recycling systems still need investment. Green technology is still underfunded. Many in power are still reluctant to act unless it serves their interests. And too many people still believe that small acts of stewardship aren't enough.

But I know better.

I know that every action matters. That every seed planted can grow—even in the snow. That every child who hears the message might one day be the person who leads the next fight. That's how legacies are built—not in grand gestures, but in thousands of purposeful, quiet acts repeated over time.

If you're reading this because you've taken up the mantle in your own life, in your own neighbourhood, then I want to tell you this: **don't let go**. Even when it feels like no one's listening. Even when the systems around you make it hard. Stay rooted. Keep showing up. Because change is not an explosion—it's erosion. It wears down resistance little by little until the cliff gives way.

So yes, I've faced setbacks. I've dealt with the weight of bureaucracy and the sting of being underestimated. But here I am—*still standing, still pushing, still believing.* And not just believing in myself—but in you. In us. In the movement that started as one man's mission and has now become a shared promise.

The promise that we won't quit.

Not today. Not tomorrow.

Not ever.

That's how you win the long game.

You stay in it—until the world bends.

Chapter 18

The Job is Not Done

People sometimes ask me if I feel like I've done enough.

They look at the years I've poured into this work—the protests, the campaigns, the late-night planning sessions, the speeches to rooms both full and empty. They see the bans, the renamed days, the reusable bags, the movement that once felt like a whisper now marching with undeniable force. And they ask, "Do you feel finished?"

Let me be clear: **I am not done**.

Not even close.

Because the Earth is not done hurting. Our rivers still run tainted. Our air still burns in the lungs of children who had no say in the industries built around them. Our oceans still churn with plastic and the silent screams of wildlife trapped in human waste are still heard. Forests fall. Ice melts. And we continue to move as if there's time to spare.

So no, I don't feel finished.

I feel *called*. Every day.

Called to keep pushing. To keep speaking. To keep showing up in places that were never built for people like me and still daring to take space. To fight not just for the planet—but for the soul of the people living on it.

This journey began with me—a boy with a basket on a Jamaican farm, learning how to carry the impossible.

But it's no longer just about me.

It's not about the petitions I've filed or the campaigns I've led. It's not about plastic bags or blue bins or even the name change from 'Garbage Day' to 'Recycle Day'. It's about *legacy*. It's about *you*. It's about what we choose to do with the time we have left and the world we've been given.

I've watched eyes light up when a child understands composting for the first time. I've seen people in suits and steel-toed boots alike come together over a shared mission to clean up a riverbank. I've listened to youth demand that their future be taken seriously, and I've nodded through tears as they said the words I longed to hear for decades: *"We are ready now."*

That's the moment I've been working towards. Not retirement. Not recognition. **Readiness**.

Because this was never just my fight to finish. It was always about lighting a path others could walk too—so that when I step aside, the road remains lit.

To the reader, let me say this: whether you've been in this fight for decades or you're only just beginning to open your eyes, you belong in this story. You don't need a title. You don't need a perfect plan. You need conviction. You need compassion. You need courage.

The Earth doesn't require your perfection. It requires your participation.

Look around at your neighbourhood, your backyard, your morning routine. What can you change? What can you do better? Who can you influence?

Start there. Start *now*.

Don't wait for a leader. Don't wait for a government memo or a perfect set of conditions. If you're waiting for permission to care, I'm giving it to you: **go**. Care loudly. Care recklessly. Care in ways that inspire and disrupt and make people uncomfortable enough to think differently.

Because the job is not done.

The oceans still need defenders. The forests still need protectors. The soil still needs stewards. And our communities—especially the most vulnerable among us—still need champions who are not afraid to connect the dots between environmental justice and human dignity.

This is not a passing interest. It is a **lifelong vow**.

I will continue to speak. To write. To advocate. To resist. Until my last breath, I will fight for this Earth.

But I no longer fight alone.

I see you. I see the torch in your hand, flickering, waiting. And I'm telling you: it's time to run with it.

Because we are not just saving the planet.

We are saving *each other*.

So let this be our pact: that we will rise every day with a renewed sense of duty, that we will love this planet fiercely and urgently, and that we will never, *ever*, confuse progress with completion.

The job is not done.

But together, we are just getting started.

Chapter 19

Letter to The Next Generation

You don't know me yet—not in the way you know your mentors, teachers, or friends. But I've spent a lifetime fighting for the world you're walking into. And though I may not be there when you reach the milestones we've only dreamed of, I want you to know this: I believed in you before you ever arrived.

I believed in your capacity to care.

I believed in your courage to speak up.

And most of all, I believed in your right to inherit a world that's liveable, equitable, and full of wonder.

If this letter reaches you when you're still figuring out who you are or what you stand for, I hope it helps you realize that your voice is never too small, and your actions are never too late. The world you inherit may come with broken systems and heavy burdens, but it also comes with open doors, waiting to be walked through by bold souls like you.

Here's what I want you to do:

Learn the names of the trees in your neighbourhood. Watch how they respond to wind and drought. Understand that they've been here longer than most buildings, and they carry wisdom we've ignored for too long.

Speak to your elders—not just your grandparents, but those who've walked before you and fought different battles. Their stories are roadmaps, even when their methods may not be your own.

Ask uncomfortable questions. If something seems unjust, unkind, or unnecessary—challenge it. Systems are built by people, and they can be rebuilt by people too.

Show up to places where decisions are made, even if you feel like you don't belong. Sit in the room. Take notes. Ask questions. Then come back the next time with ten more people who look and sound like you.

Be stewards, not owners. The land, the air, the rivers—none of it belongs to us. We are caretakers for a moment in time. Leave things better than you found them.

Build community—not just online, but in your physical spaces. Knock on your neighbour's door. Start a conversation. Offer help without being asked. A sustainable world cannot survive without connection.

Never let cynicism convince you that the fight is useless. There will be setbacks. There will be losses. But progress does not die with defeat. It grows in the cracks, like dandelions in the sidewalk.

And lastly—dream. Not small, practical dreams. But wild ones. Dream of cities without landfills, schools powered by sunlight, grocery stores with local food in every aisle, rivers so clean you can drink straight from their currents. Dream of a world that does not punish the poor or forget the voiceless. Dream until the dream becomes a blueprint.

This letter isn't just a collection of ideas. It's a passing of the torch. We've carried it as far as we could. It's burning still, but it needs your hands now.

Take it.

Run with it.

And whatever you do—don't let it go.

With trust in your light,

Don Woodstock

White plastic tangled in trees near a high-rise building

Chapter 20

Faith Over Fear

I didn't set out to change a country.

Let me make that clear.

I wasn't chasing national headlines or drafting policy in the back of my mind. I didn't see a movement. I saw a mess. I saw plastic bags stuck in trees, garbage bins overflowing and garbage in the streets, and people too tired or too uninformed to care. All I wanted—*all I truly wanted*—was to make my city better. Cleaner. Healthier. More sustainable for the next generation.

I started by trying to change the people around me.

That's it.

If I could just get them to see what I saw... if I could just get them to understand that recycling wasn't some government inconvenience but an act of love for their community... I believed they would change their behaviour. And they did. *Slowly*. But they did. Because when you shift someone's mindset, their lifestyle starts to follow.

But that kind of work doesn't come without resistance. It doesn't come without loneliness. It doesn't come without people looking at you sideways, brushing you off, laughing behind closed doors, and calling you delusional for thinking a Jamaican-born man with no title, no budget, no elected office, no ringing endorsement by the political elites, nor the people who claim to have the city's best-interest at heart could change how a city treats its trash. Just your average everyday neighbour.

They doubted me. They ignored me. Some even mocked me.

But I didn't waver. Not for a minute.

Because I had something they couldn't see. I had **faith**.

You see when you walk in faith, you don't need a crowd to believe in your dream. You just need *conviction*. You don't need permission to start. You just need purpose. And even when fear creeps in, even when it whispers that you're out of your depth, that you're going to fail, that no one's listening—you keep walking.

I live by something simple: To face your **F.E.A.R. — False Evidence Appearing Real**.

Fear is often nothing more than an illusion, dressed up to look like logic. Fear is the voice that says, *You're not qualified. You're not welcome. No one cares.* But those voices - they're cowards. And I've never given cowards the power to dictate my next step.

Because when you're fuelled by faith, you understand that you don't have to see the whole staircase—you just need to take the next step.

I took that step the day I walked into Winnipeg City Hall with a proposal to rename "Garbage Day" to "Recycle Day."

I took it again when I walked into school gyms with nothing but a tote bag and a conviction that even children could become environmental warriors.

And I took it every time I stood alone—outside the spotlight, outside the system—believing something better was possible when everyone else was content to let things stay the same.

Faith is what kept me going when meetings were cut short.

Faith is what held me upright when emails went unanswered.

Faith is what warmed my heart when winter winds told me to go home.

And faith—*not politics, not privilege*—is what carried this message far beyond the blocks I first canvassed. I didn't change Canada. *Canada changed because people started changing their minds.* That was the real miracle.

You see, people think movements begin with masses. But most often, they start with **one person** who refuses to bow to fear and dares to say, *"This isn't good enough. We can do better."*

I was that one.

I wasn't a celebrity. I wasn't a scholar. I was just a man with a dream of a better city—*for all of us.* A place where clean air wasn't a luxury. A place where you didn't have to teach your children to walk around garbage but to care enough to clean it up.

My faith told me it could happen.

My faith told me it *would* happen—if I just stayed unrelenting.

And I did.

Not because the road was easy, but because the reward was worth it. Seeing blue bins lined up & down back lanes, seeing reusable bags in the hands of shoppers, hearing children talk about composting at school—*that's faith fulfilled!*" It was about standing in the gap when no one else would. Playing my part in the sustainable approach even if I was the only one showing up to do it some days.

Faith, for me, is grounded in my belief in God as it was taught to me by my late mother & grandfather. It is the faith that does not require you to find 50,000 people to walk with you. But you and your convictions, with God, makes all the difference in the world. Knowing very well that God's word said, "Yay though you walk in the valley of the Shadow of Death, fear no evil because I am with you, always!"

If you're reading this and you've ever felt dismissed, if you've ever had a dream that people around you don't understand, *keep going anyways.* Their doubt doesn't define you. Their silence doesn't stop you. And their fear? It's not yours to carry.

Because one thing I know is true: **faith moves mountains—but only after it moves you**.

And the best thing you can do with your faith is walk it out—day by day, step by step, bin by bin.

You never know who's watching.

You never know how far it will reach.

I didn't set out to change Canada.

But my faith in God made sure I did.

And you can do the same!

Epilogue

The Soil Remembers

There is something deeply humbling about writing the final words of a life's work. It feels like closing the gate to a field you've spent decades planting, weeding, watering, and defending from storms. You look out one last time and ask yourself the only question that matters: *Did it grow?*

As I reflect on my journey—born in Jamaica's sun-drenched soil, raised by a grandfather who taught me the value of patience, and shaped by the people of Winnipeg who challenged me to dream bigger and bolder—I can say with both exhaustion and pride: yes, it grew.

But what grew was never just mine. The seeds were sown by many hands. Some carried by the wind. Some pressed deep into the earth by hardship. Others buried for years, waiting for the right season to bloom.

I did not do this work for applause. I did it for legacy. For integrity. For the deep and aching truth that our time on this earth is not just a story—it's a responsibility.

There were years when I was barely heard. When my name was misspelled, my emails left unread, my intentions misunderstood. But those years taught me the most valuable lesson of all: *you do not need to be seen to make a difference—you just need to keep showing up.*

So, I showed up.

I showed up in council chambers. I showed up in schools. I showed up at public events dressed in a foam mascot suit. I showed up to meetings where I wasn't welcome and to neighbourhoods that had been forgotten. I showed up with reusable bags, with documentaries, with song lyrics and speeches and petitions. I showed up until no one could ignore me. I showed up until change became inevitable.

And I'll tell you something else—I made peace with being misunderstood. I accepted the role of agitator. Not because I enjoy the discomfort, but because I've seen what happens when good people stay silent out of fear of making waves.

The oceans are rising. We need waves.

As I write this, the world is shifting. Climate disasters no longer feel like distant forecasts—they are lived experiences. Cities are choking. Forests are burning. And yet, people are waking up. I've seen the awakening in real time—in the eyes of children who now know what composting means, in the actions of parents who stopped buying single-use plastics, in the businesses turning rooftops into gardens and parking lots into food forests.

This work is not theoretical. It's practical. It's visible. And it is *urgent.*

But urgency is not panic. Urgency is clarity. And clarity is what I offer you now.

We are not too late. The clock is not our enemy. Indifference is.

We must remain uncomfortable with injustice. With waste. With laziness dressed as tradition. We must dare to challenge what we've normalized and ask: "Does it still serve us—or is it killing us slowly?"

If there is one regret I have, it is this: I wish more people had believed in themselves sooner. I wish more individuals understood the power of *one voice*. We are often told to wait, to study more, to prove our worth, to build coalitions before we act. But in that waiting, the world burns. We need doers. We need people willing to fail forward, to try imperfectly, only to rise again.

Because there is no perfect saviour coming. There is only us. And the Earth cannot wait for our confidence to catch up.

I hope, long after I'm gone, that these words outlive me. That somewhere, someone will pick up this book and realize they're not alone in their passion. That persistence is not just a virtue—it is a weapon against decay. That their voice matters not because it is loud, but because it is consistent.

I hope teachers will use this book to teach courage. That activists will use it to rest their weary hearts and find strength in knowing others have fought too. That elected officials will be reminded of their duty not to maintain power, but to serve the greater good. That ordinary people will be reminded there's no such thing as "ordinary."

I was never a polished politician. I was never rich. I didn't have the perfect connections. But I had two things: **conviction and clarity**. And I never lost sight of what we were trying to protect. The soil. The water. The children.

And the soil remembers.

It remembers how we treated it. It remembers every drop of rain, every footstep, every hand that reached down to pull a weed or plant a seed. It remembers kindness. And it remembers neglect. It remembers.

So will history.

One day, people will look back on this era and ask, "What did they do when the world was gasping?" Let the answer be this: *They acted. They fought. They listened. They changed.*

Let our footprints be light and our legacy deep.

To my family—thank you for allowing me to pour myself into this cause. To the believers who stood beside me even when the crowd walked away—you are the reason hope survives. To my critics—thank you. You made me sharper. Stronger. More relentless. And to every citizen who took even one step toward a greener world—you are part of the story now. And it is a beautiful one.

This is not a goodbye.

This is a passing of the spade. The garden is yours now. The work, unfinished—but bursting with potential.

I have planted.

Now it's your turn to water.

With resolve,

Don Woodstock, Unrelenting.